D1512268

A New Path

Gail Chianese

AnniesFiction.com

Books in The Inn at Magnolia Harbor series

Where Hope Blooms
Safe Harbor
Binding Vows
Tender Melody
At Summer's End
Mending the Past
Kindred Blessings
Grateful Hearts
Christmas Gifts
Joyful Beginnings
Love's Surprise
Season of Renewal
Drawing Hope
A Guiding Promise
Cherished Legacy
Garden of Secrets
Sweet Wishes
August Retreat
A New Path
Autumn's Spell
Treasured Harvest
Comfort and Joy
A Time to Celebrate
Forever Starts Today

Library of Congress-in-Publication Data
A New Path / by Gail Chianese
p. cm.
I. Title
                    2020944673

AnniesFiction.com
(800) 282-6643
The Inn at Magnolia Harbor™
Series Creator: Shari Lohner
Editor: Lorie Jones
Cover Illustrator: Bonnie Leick

10 11 12 13 14 | Printed in South Korea | 9 8 7 6 5 4 3 2

1

Melinda

Melinda Faye Rainey steered her trusty blue sedan onto the flower-lined driveway leading up to the Magnolia Harbor Inn. As she regarded the magnificent inn, she got distracted and had to brake hard before she drove off the road.

Having lived her entire life in the South—first Montgomery, Alabama, and now Roswell, Georgia—Melinda had seen her share of antebellum mansions. She couldn't go for a drive without passing at least one historical building, and most were abandoned and decrepit. But the Magnolia Harbor Inn was gleaming white in the sunshine, surrounded by oaks draped with Spanish moss, dogwoods, and magnolias, many still in bloom. It felt like stepping back in time to a quieter world.

In other words, it was exactly what Melinda needed to clear the clutter from her mind and get her head on straight. Of course, it was the exact opposite of what her bank account needed now that she was officially unemployed.

She still couldn't believe that after more than twenty-five years of exemplary service, the company had let her go. When her supervisor had handed her the paperwork, she'd laughed, sure it was a practical joke. It had been the first of April and crunch time for taxes. However, he hadn't laughed with her. When Melinda glanced around the office and noticed her coworkers wouldn't meet her eyes, she knew it wasn't a joke.

But Melinda had held her head high and refused to cry. No

respectable Southern woman would dare cry in public and ruin her makeup. At least that was what her mom always said. Thankfully, the company had given Melinda two weeks' notice and six weeks' severance. She'd deserved no less after all she'd done for them over the years.

She'd also figured another job would appear with the snap of her fingers. There had to be a market for an experienced accountant with an impeccable record. But time was proving her wrong.

Five months later, she still hadn't landed a new job.

Sighing, Melinda parked her car and got out. She tugged her suitcase out of the trunk, then stumbled backward as the weight hit her in the middle of the chest, nearly toppling her to the ground. It was big and contained way too many clothes, but she honestly had no idea how she'd be spending her vacation. She hadn't really thought the trip through when she'd booked her stay at the inn. A former client had mentioned the bed-and-breakfast a few times, and when Melinda saw the pictures online, the place had called out to her.

In person it was even more inviting. The grounds were beautiful and immaculately manicured, like a park or an oasis. Maybe she'd spend some time strolling along the paths. Good thing she'd brought her tennis shoes.

Then again, there were a few inviting rocking chairs on the front porch, and she gave them a wistful sigh as she climbed the stairs. Melinda could easily picture herself sipping a cup of tea as the sun rose, greeting the day. Or maybe she'd while the day away with a book as the world passed by.

As Melinda opened the door, a small bell jingled. She stepped into a pristine foyer with marble floors and the most breathtaking crystal chandelier overhead. Melinda parked her suitcase and peered up the grand staircase, expecting someone to greet her at any moment. "Hello?" she called.

As the seconds ticked by on a nearby grandfather clock, Melinda began to feel uneasy. The place didn't seem like an inn but rather someone's home, and she had walked inside uninvited.

A lovely woman in her midforties entered the room. She was dressed casually in jeans, a short-sleeve tunic, and sandals.

Melinda's unease instantly slipped away with the woman's kind smile.

"Welcome to the Magnolia Harbor Inn," she said. "I'm Grace Porter, one of the owners."

"I'm Melinda Faye Rainey, but you can call me Melinda. I have a reservation."

"Yes, you do," Grace said as she went to the reception desk. "I have your registration here."

"Your inn is gorgeous," Melinda remarked. "The pictures online are gorgeous, but they still don't do it justice." If a picture was worth a thousand words, then the real deal was worth twice that.

"Thank you. That's so kind." Grace glanced around the room, then shook her head in what appeared to be resignation. "I'll need you to sign this." She handed Melinda the form, but her attention seemed to be once again pulled in a different direction.

As Melinda took the document and signed it, she wondered if she'd arrived at an inconvenient time. Technically, she was a bit early for check-in. "I feel that I should apologize for arriving early," she said, returning the form. "I've probably thrown you off your schedule, but I was so excited to start my vacation, and traffic was surprisingly light."

"There's no reason to apologize. Your room is ready." Grace frowned. "Please excuse my bad manners. I'm afraid I've misplaced a key, and for the life of me, I can't figure out where it could be."

"Have you checked the freezer?" Melinda asked.

Grace raised her eyebrows. "No, I can't say that I have. Do you normally find lost items there?"

"More often than I care to admit," Melinda said, leaning forward. "When I'm tired, I tend to reach for a carton of ice cream instead of cooking, and I've found my reading glasses frozen the next morning. Or my car keys. Once I even found a handheld calculator."

"Oh, goodness. I'll have to take a peek," Grace said. "Do you mind my asking what is it that you do?"

"I'm an accountant." Or was. Melinda wasn't sure what she'd be next. Maybe she could turn her home into a boutique bed-and-breakfast. It had a few empty bedrooms that were collecting dust. But she didn't know the first thing about being an innkeeper. Then again, once upon a time, she hadn't known anything about being an accountant either. "It must be wonderful owning this inn."

"It is," Grace said. "My sister, Charlotte Wylde, and I run it together."

"A family business," Melinda said. "How nice."

"Would you care for a glass of iced tea?" Grace asked. "I have a fresh pitcher in the living room."

"That sounds great." Melinda left her suitcase in the foyer and followed her hostess.

The living room was done in neutral tones with comfortable chairs and two sofas set up for conversation with a view of the lake and a fireplace, currently not in use. Floor-to-ceiling windows provided an unobstructed view of the immaculate grounds. The room was worthy of a magazine cover.

"Please have a seat." Grace walked over to a table and poured two glasses of tea.

Melinda sat down on the sofa that faced the lake.

"So, what brings you to Magnolia Harbor?" Grace handed Melinda a glass and took a seat on the sofa across from her. "Are you here for the barbecue festival?"

"Barbecue festival?" Melinda echoed, holding her glass a few inches over the crystal coaster. It sounded messy, and Melinda didn't do messy.

Grace nodded, then took a sip of her tea. "The festival is held in the next town over. It's a lot of fun. Basically, it's a weeklong feast with pie-eating and baking contests and of course the barbecue competition. There are also carnival rides and games as well as booths of craft vendors and a band."

Melinda didn't want to insult her hostess, so she hesitated, searching for the right response. Even though it sounded like a good time, pie-eating contests, barbecue sauce, and flimsy paper plates all usually led to one thing, and that was Melinda spilling food down the front of her shirt. "That sounds great. Actually, I'm here to clear my head and get some perspective. I'm at a crossroads in my career."

"I've been there," Grace admitted. "It can be a bit daunting."

"I'm hoping it will help to get away for a little while," Melinda said. "I plan to exercise and spend some time in the fresh air. To tell you the truth, I feel like I'm seventeen again and trying to decide what to do with my life." She cringed. "I know that sounds silly."

Somehow Melinda remembered it being a whole lot easier the first time around. She'd been good with numbers, and her high school business teacher had recommended her to a company in need of help. Before Melinda knew it, she'd transitioned from working part-time after school to full-time after her high school graduation. And there she'd stayed for many years.

She stared down at her feet, too embarrassed to meet Grace's eyes. It was obvious that her hostess didn't know what Melinda was talking about. Grace ran a lovely inn, the perfect blend of elegance and hospitality.

"I've been in your shoes before," Grace said. "I didn't always own an inn."

"Really?" Melinda glanced around the beautiful room, shocked. The inn was so warm and inviting that she'd assumed the sisters had grown up here or at least worked in the business before opening the inn. "What did you do?"

"I worked for a marketing firm in Charleston for nearly twenty years," Grace answered. "I enjoyed it, but I got burned out. When I switched careers, it brought a fair share of scary moments and some sleepless nights. It was a big risk, and at the time, I had a teenager to raise on my own."

"That's amazing. Please forgive me for being so nosy, but how did you decide on becoming an innkeeper?" To Melinda, the choice was as far removed from marketing as accounting was, so maybe there was hope she'd find a new calling.

Before Grace could respond, there was a soft bark, followed by the clicking of nails on the marble floor. An adorable bundle of fur ran straight to Melinda, plopping down on the floor and gazing up at her with pleading brown eyes.

Grace smiled. "Meet Winston. The inn's official welcoming party."

The dog yipped and lifted his paw.

"Oh, he's so sweet." Melinda held out a hand to let the shih tzu mix sniff her before shaking his paw.

Winston stuck his head under her hand.

Melinda laughed, then spent a couple of minutes talking to the dog and giving him all her attention and love. "Please forgive me," she said to Grace. "I've always wanted a dog, but I've never had the time. You were going to tell me why you decided to open an inn."

Grace waved off her apology. She was probably used to playing second fiddle to Winston with guests. "I wanted something a little slower paced that also gave me more freedom to do what I enjoy. I love to provide a haven for others and give them a restful environment so they feel refreshed and restored as they go back to their everyday lives. And meeting new people such as yourself is so much more enjoyable than being in an office. Plus, I get to work with my sister."

"It sounds like a great choice," Melinda said.

"It's a good fit." Grace stood and scanned the room, probably still trying to figure out where she'd put the lost key. "I'm sure you'll find your niche too. Give it time."

"Thank you," Melinda said. "I hope so."

"I imagine after your long drive you'd like to get settled into your room," Grace said. "We have you in the Dogwood Suite. It has a private bath and a view of Lake Haven."

"That sounds wonderful." Melinda grabbed her suitcase in the foyer and followed Grace and Winston to the second floor.

Grace opened the door of the Dogwood Suite and stepped aside, allowing Melinda to enter.

Melinda gave a deep sigh, feeling her shoulders relax at the sight. The room was impressive. It featured a king-size bed with two chairs facing the fireplace. A lovely desk sat in the corner, offering the ideal place to work on her life plans should inspiration strike. French doors opened onto a veranda, where she could sit and enjoy the sunrise or sunset over the lake and listen to the birds and cicadas play their sweet music.

"We have hospitality hour every night from six to seven," Grace said. "Charlotte prepares the appetizers, and she's an incredible chef. Please join us tonight on the back veranda."

"I'll be there," Melinda said.

"Let me know if you need anything," Grace said. "I hope you like your room."

Melinda smiled at her hostess. "I love it. It's exactly what I need."

2

Tiffany

As Tiffany Jackson slowly drove through downtown Magnolia Harbor, she took in the sights—or rather made note of what was missing. Sure, the small town was charming. The cobblestone streets were lined with majestic old trees and quaint shops. But where were the chain stores and coffee shops?

Well, there was a place called the Dragonfly Coffee Shop that appeared promising. A waitress chatted with customers seated outside as they enjoyed the beautiful September weather. Definitely not something the chain store employees had time to do. Still, Magnolia Harbor, South Carolina, was a long way from Atlanta, Georgia.

What did her aunt, Laura Devereux, do when she wanted to go to the movies or had cravings for Indian food at ten o'clock at night? Charming was great, but what about restaurant and entertainment options and culture?

Magnolia Harbor seemed to be everything home wasn't. Living here would have driven her mom nuts. Donna Jackson had been all about life's varied experiences.

Maybe her mother and her aunt were exact opposites, and that was why her aunt had settled down in such a sleepy little town. It also might explain why Tiffany had lived for thirty years without knowing her mother even had a sister.

Then again, perhaps her aunt had been the smarter one. What would Tiffany's life have been like had they lived in a place like Magnolia Harbor instead of moving to Marietta? She had to admit the lack of traffic was a welcome relief. She'd already felt a dramatic drop in her stress level.

Tiffany's thoughts returned to her mother. She had been larger than life, full of love and wisdom and lots of laughter. She'd taught her daughter to treasure everything that life brought her way, to never stop learning, to always give of herself, to help those in need, and to love.

Right up until the end, when cancer took her life.

But Tiffany didn't want to dwell on the sad days. The days filled with sickness and forced smiles. She knew that wasn't what her mother would want either.

Instead, Tiffany focused on happier times when her family was whole and together. She fondly recalled when her parents took her to museums, concerts, plays, and the ballet. She would cherish those memories for the rest of her life. They made her remember who she was and where she came from. Someday she hoped to be able to pass those precious gifts on to her own children.

As Tiffany drove out of town and along Lake Haven Road toward the inn, she imagined what it would have been like to grow up in a house on the shore. Her dad would have gone fishing every morning before work. Her mom would have planted flowers facing the lake. They would have had a rowboat tied to a dock they could have dived off for a cool summer swim and sat on to dangle their toes into the water during a late-night chat. As much as her parents relished the hustle and bustle of city living, she could easily picture them here in this slow country world.

Tiffany couldn't help but wonder if she would still have her dad if they'd lived here. He'd been a cop, killed by a drunk driver while on duty one night. She couldn't imagine this area saw much crime. People probably stumbled home from the local bar, if they even had one, or bummed a ride with a friend or a neighbor. She'd heard about small towns like this one, where they all knew and watched out for each other.

However, nothing would have changed her mother's battle with cancer or the outcome. That much she was sure of. The horrible disease didn't care where a person lived.

Pushing the maudlin thoughts away, Tiffany drove down the pretty drive to a gorgeous mansion that would be her home for almost a week. The majestic trees created canopies of shade across the lush green lawn. Sweet magnolias scented the air as birds chirped a merry little tune in their branches.

If all attempts with her aunt failed, Tiffany could spend her days lounging around the spectacular inn and working on her tan. A luxury she hadn't had time for this past year.

Suddenly, the thought of meeting her aunt—a woman she hadn't even known existed until two weeks ago—sent butterflies fluttering in her stomach. What if Laura was crazy? Every family had one relative they secretly hoped would skip family functions. What if her aunt turned out to be that person?

Tiffany's imagination spun away with one scenario after another. What if her aunt wasn't a quirky embarrassment to the family? What if she was dangerous? No, that wasn't possible. Tiffany's mother would have never asked her to do anything that put her in jeopardy. But what if her mom hadn't known? It had been more than thirty years since her mother had seen her sister. For all Tiffany knew, she could walk into Laura's cabin—why she thought it was a cabin was beyond her—and never be seen again.

Taking a deep breath, she exited the car and retrieved her suitcase from the trunk. There had to be a reasonable explanation for why the sisters hadn't spoken in three decades. She would ask her aunt about it. It was probably a simple case of life taking them in different directions.

Tiffany shook her head at the ridiculous notion. Sisters didn't lose touch for decades over that.

As she climbed the porch steps, she wondered if she should invite her aunt to meet her somewhere public instead of showing up unannounced on her doorstep. She recalled how welcoming the Dragonfly Coffee Shop had been. Perhaps that would be a good meeting place. Even if Laura didn't show up, Tiffany could sit inside the shop with a cup of coffee and lose herself in a book for a few hours. It had been months since she'd had time to relax.

Tiffany opened the door and heard a bell jingle. She entered the elaborate foyer and felt her jaw drop as she took in the sparkling chandelier overhead and the curved banister, with its intricate scrollwork gracing the railings, leading to the second floor. She wouldn't want to dust this place, but it was certainly stunning. The pictures on the website were amazing, but the actual mansion was ten times more elegant, more polished, more . . . everything.

It was definitely not the kind of inn where Tiffany normally stayed. Left on her own, she would have booked some midrange chain hotel in Charleston. Thankfully, she'd listened to her boyfriend, Chris Russell, and chosen the Magnolia Harbor Inn instead. It was simply divine, and she hadn't even seen her room yet.

Tiffany walked over to the unmanned reception desk and set her suitcase down on the floor. It was still a little before check-in, but she'd been so nervous about the drive and meeting her aunt that her foot might have been a bit heavy on the accelerator.

Now that she was here, she could relax somewhat. Maybe take a nap. Get a lay of the land. Quiz her hostesses to see if they knew her aunt. All the calm she'd managed to find a minute ago zipped right out the window as she started thinking about why she was on this trip. If only it were a regular vacation.

She definitely needed one after the last few months.

Even with Chris gearing up for another deployment soon, Tiffany wanted some time away from home to . . . what? Grieve? She'd been doing that for months as she'd watched the vibrant woman who'd brought her into the world wither away to nothing but a shell of a human. No, Tiffany had already cried her eyes out. She'd railed at the world and all its unjust laws of nature. She'd bargained and begged.

Not that any of those things had made a difference. Her mom was still gone, and Tiffany was technically alone. The only family she had left was a mysterious aunt she knew absolutely nothing about and was terrified to meet.

No, this vacation would serve as a time to regroup.

The sounds of tiny nails clicking across the marble floor caught her attention.

Tiffany glanced down into a pair of warm brown eyes and instantly fell in love.

Her suitor turned in a circle and then barked three times before extending a furry brown paw to her.

"Oh, he's so precious." Bending down, she took the proffered paw and shook it.

The dog gave up all pretenses of formality and climbed into her arms, then gave her kisses.

"I see you've met Winston," a woman said as she entered the room. "He loves making new friends."

Tiffany laughed. "Now this is how every hotel should greet their guests."

"Trust me, Winston does his best. You can put him down if you like. Otherwise, he'll be happy to stay like that for your entire visit."

"That would be fine with me." Tiffany stood and kissed Winston's head. "My mom had a dog like this. I guess he's mine now." She buried her nose in Winston's fur. "She recently passed."

"I know it doesn't ease the pain," the woman said, "but I'm so sorry for your loss."

For the first time in days, Tiffany didn't feel as if those were empty words spoken because it was the right thing to do. It was like this woman Tiffany had just met understood what she was going through and genuinely felt for her. "Thank you. I haven't had a dog in years. Maybe Winston can help break me in during my stay. Show me the ropes of being a dog parent."

"Well, he's always up for a good snuggle, and he loves to play fetch. He even knows a few tricks." The woman smiled. "By the way, welcome to the Magnolia Harbor Inn. I'm Grace Porter, one of the owners. You must be Tiffany Jackson."

"Yes, I am. Sorry I got distracted, but I have a feeling that happens a lot when your guests meet this adorable little one." She gently set Winston on the floor.

"All the time," Grace said, grinning. "How about we get you checked in? I'm sure you're tired after your drive."

"I could use a nap," Tiffany admitted. "Honestly, I didn't sleep much last night."

"We've put you in the Buttercup Suite," Grace said, giving her a registration form. "It has a king-size bed, with a full view of the lake, and the breeze is very soothing. At night, you can hear the water lapping against the shore. It puts me right to sleep. It also has a private bath. I think it's exactly what you'll need for a good night's rest."

Tiffany signed the registration form, then slid it across the desk to her hostess. "I hope so. I have a big day tomorrow."

Grace headed toward the stairs with Winston on her heels. "Your room is on the second floor."

Tiffany grabbed her suitcase and followed her up the stairs.

"Are you here for business or pleasure?" Grace asked.

Tiffany hadn't considered how to answer questions about her trip. If she said she was visiting family, then people would expect that she'd be excited and would actually know her aunt. How could she explain that Laura Devereux was a big mystery and that meeting her was more of an obligation? It was a dying woman's last wish.

Tiffany had to say something, especially if she was hoping Grace would have some kind of information for her. "A little bit of both."

"It's always nice if you can add pleasure to a business trip," Grace remarked, unlocking the door to the Buttercup Suite.

Tiffany entered the room. It was richly appointed with a huge, high bed. It was a good thing she was tall, or she might have needed a step stool to get into it each night. There was a fireplace, which probably didn't get much use in South Carolina, and it probably wouldn't during her stay, but it added a cozy touch. Her favorite part of the room was the overstuffed chair in the corner. It was the ideal place to curl up with a book and unwind.

"Please join us for our nightly hospitality hour from six to seven," Grace said. "It'll be served on the back veranda. My sister, Charlotte Wylde, is an amazing chef, and she's making some special appetizers for tonight."

"I'll be there," Tiffany said. She figured it was now or never if she was going to ask about her aunt. "Do you happen to know Laura Devereux in Magnolia Harbor?"

Grace leaned against the doorjamb and crossed her arms. "That name doesn't ring a bell, but I can ask my sister. Better yet, I can ask Winnie Bennett, my aunt. She's lived here for a long time, and she knows pretty much everyone in the area."

"There's no need to go to any trouble." Tiffany dropped into the overstuffed chair and picked Winston up, snuggling him. How was she supposed to admit that Laura was the aunt she'd never met?

"It's no trouble," Grace said.

"I was curious because I want to be prepared and make a good impression," Tiffany said. "Laura is my aunt, and she doesn't know I'm coming to see her. I don't even think she knows I exist."

"Really?" Grace asked, obviously surprised.

"I didn't find out about her until two weeks ago," Tiffany admitted. "Now I have to visit her, so I was hoping for a little information about her before I go. But what if she doesn't want to meet me?"

Grace smiled. "I'm sure she'll love meeting you. Why wouldn't she?"

Tiffany tried to return the smile, but it felt weak on her face. She wondered why her aunt hadn't talked to her own sister for thirty years. And how would a woman like that react to her sister's daughter showing up on her doorstep uninvited?

Grace

After showing Tiffany to her room, Grace Porter headed downstairs to her own private quarters. For once, she was thankful they weren't booked solid. One of their guests had canceled her reservation at the last minute.

Their third and final guest, Ryan Scoville, wouldn't be arriving for a little while. Ryan had been a yearly visitor since Grace and Charlotte had opened the inn, and Grace always enjoyed catching up with him.

Winston had reluctantly left Tiffany and trailed Grace into her room. He plopped into his dog bed after giving it a thorough fluffing.

"Busy day, pal?" Grace chuckled as she searched her dresser drawers for the missing shed key. "I know greeting the guests is hard work, but you do an outstanding job making everyone feel welcome. Charlotte and I appreciate it. Maybe you'll even find an extra treat in your dinner bowl tonight."

"What is Winston being rewarded for now?" Charlotte asked from the doorway.

Grace shut one drawer and moved to the next. "Both Tiffany Jackson and Melinda Rainey fell helplessly in love with Winston today. If nothing else, they'll give us a five-star rating because of him."

"I have a feeling they'll give us a good review for more than our greeting party." Charlotte watched her for a few minutes with a bemused expression. "What in the world are you searching for? You've been tossing pillows and such around all day."

Grace dropped into a chair, letting out an exasperated sigh.

"The key to the storage shed. It's not hanging up in the kitchen where it's supposed to be. I've looked everywhere. You don't think I accidentally locked it in the shed when I put the kayaks away last week, do you?"

"No, because Oliver was here yesterday, and he put the rakes back in the shed after mowing the lawn." Charlotte tilted her head. "He might have forgotten to leave the key."

Two Green Thumbs was the best lawn care company around. Grace couldn't imagine Oliver Nichols, the owner, forgetting something like returning the shed key, but stranger things had happened. "Maybe I'll give him a call. Could you also keep an eye out for my thimble? I can't seem to remember where I left that either, although I'd swear it was here on the table the other night. If I didn't know better, I'd say the inn was haunted."

Charlotte laughed and headed into the kitchen.

Grace followed, inhaling the enticing aroma of melting cheese. Her sister was a renowned chef, and she'd written a few best-selling cookbooks. Whatever Charlotte was making for this evening's hospitality hour would be delicious.

"If we had a ghost, don't you think we would have known about it before now?" Charlotte handed Grace a glass of lemonade, then turned to the oven to check whatever was baking.

The kitchen door swung open before Grace could answer, and both sisters smiled when their aunt bustled into the room.

"Hello, my dears," Winnie said. "I was out for a walk and thought I'd pop in and see how things were coming along with the new guests."

"What a nice surprise," Grace said as she poured another glass of lemonade.

"I agree." Charlotte hugged their aunt.

Grace handed Winnie the glass and slid onto a stool at the

marble-topped island. "We have a light list this week. Only three guests. Melinda Rainey is at a career crossroads. I got the feeling she might be a bit lost in the fog right now."

"We'll see if we can't help shine the light on to the right path for her," Winnie said, sitting down next to Grace.

Charlotte retrieved a container of cookies. She removed one, set it on a plate, and handed it to Winnie. "Try it and tell me what you think."

Winnie took a bite of the cookie and smiled. "It's wonderful. Not too sweet. Nice hint of cinnamon and nutmeg. Moist. Pumpkin?"

"Sweet potato." Charlotte pulled a tray of cookies out of the oven and set them on the cooling rack. "I used a maple frosting on them but only a drizzle so it doesn't overpower the cookie."

Winnie put the cookie on the plate. "Oh no, that's too much sugar for me."

"Here's the best part," Charlotte said. "The cookies and the frosting are both sugar-free. I also used coconut flour and just enough sweet potato to give them flavor, so the carb count should be low enough that you don't have to worry about your diabetes."

"They're sugar-free, and they taste like this?" Winnie asked. "I'll take a dozen. Maybe you'd better send home a second dozen for your uncle because I'm not sharing mine."

The sisters laughed.

Winnie Bennett was the sweetest, most caring woman in the world who would give a complete stranger anything, but apparently, she drew the line at sharing cookies with her husband, Gus. Who could blame her when Charlotte had baked them?

"I made them especially for you *and* Gus," Charlotte said.

"Thank you," Winnie said. She took another bite of her cookie. "Now tell me about your other guests."

"Tiffany Jackson is around thirty, and she's very nice," Grace said.

"Oh, she asked if I know Laura Devereux. Does that name ring a bell for either of you?"

"Not for me." Charlotte sat down. "Did she say why she was asking?"

"Laura is her long-lost aunt," Grace replied. "Poor Tiffany seems nervous about meeting her. She's afraid Laura won't like her."

Winnie finished her cookie. "I seem to recall a Devereux in the county, but I can't place from where. I don't think she lived in Magnolia Harbor. Maybe she lived in Snellville or Lone Oaks."

"Tiffany told me that she lives in Magnolia Harbor," Grace said. "It seemed like she wanted reassurance. I'm guessing they'll become fast friends in no time."

"Probably, because I couldn't imagine it any other way with you two," Winnie said. "So, who else is on the guest list this week?"

Grace smiled. "Ryan Scoville."

"Oh, I adore Ryan. He's such a sweet man," Winnie gushed. Her tone turned serious. "But we still miss Beth."

"I can't believe it's been five years since she passed," Grace said.

"It goes by fast," Winnie said. She finished her cookie. "Although they were a bit of an odd couple."

"You know what they say—opposites attract," Charlotte said. "Look at you and Gus. He's your opposite, quiet and reserved." She laughed.

"True." Winnie hopped up from her stool, gave each sister a hug, and went to the door.

"Don't forget your cookies." Charlotte grabbed the container and passed it to her aunt.

"Thanks. Gus will love them too." Winnie paused. "Did you come up with a theme for Helen's surprise birthday party yet?"

Helen Daley was a good friend and a member of The Busy Bees, the quilting group that Winnie belonged to. Her husband was Keith Daley, the captain of the Magnolia Harbor Police

Department. Grace wanted the party for Helen to be special. She was a wonderful lady with rheumatoid arthritis, but she rarely let it slow her down. Still, she'd had some rough days lately and deserved a joyous celebration.

"Not yet," Grace said. "If you have any suggestions, I'll be anxious to hear them."

"Let me noodle on it for a while," Winnie said. "I'll stop by tonight to say hello to Ryan and meet your other guests. I can't wait to ask Ryan about a bird I spotted the other day. If you need anything before then, give me a shout."

"Thanks," Grace said. "We'll see you later."

With a wave, Winnie was out the back door and off to finish her daily walk.

"I think you made Winnie's day with those cookies," Grace said.

"I wanted to do something special for her," Charlotte said. "She does so much for us and she's done a great job managing her diabetes, but I know she misses her sweets."

"Well, it was *sweet* of you." Grace glanced around at the orderly countertops, hoping to spot the missing key. She opened the top drawer in case it had accidentally fallen inside.

"Is the key in there?" Charlotte asked. She set the cookies on the island and stirred the frosting.

"No." Grace scanned the kitchen one more time, then sighed. "I'm going to give Oliver a call. Then I'll check the music room. It's the only place I haven't looked yet."

"I'll help you as soon as I finish with the cookies."

"Thanks, but you should focus on the appetizers for tonight. I'll find it." Grace went to the reception desk and called Oliver. He told her that he'd left the shed key in the kitchen as he usually did. She thanked him and disconnected.

Grace searched the music room. She lifted every cushion, removed and replaced every throw pillow, opened and closed every drawer. She even peeked inside the baby grand piano. Still, she had no luck finding the missing shed key.

Grace was contemplating getting on her hands and knees to feel along the edges of the rug when Winston scampered into the foyer and barked.

Sure enough, a few seconds later, she heard the sound of footsteps on the front porch. By the time she entered the foyer, her third and final guest was already inside.

"Hey, Winston, old pal, how are you doing?" Ryan sat on the floor while he gave the dog a belly rub. "Have you been a good boy?"

Winston yipped as if in response.

Ryan finished playing with Winston and stood, then smiled at Grace. "It's so good to see you."

They exchanged a quick hug. He'd long ago stopped being simply a guest. Now he was a friend of the family.

"You too," Grace said. "We're always thrilled when you visit."

"How are you?" Ryan asked as he reached down to ruffle Winston's ears. "And how are Charlotte and Winnie?"

"Good," she answered. "Charlotte's in the kitchen working on tonight's hors d'oeuvres. You just missed Winnie, but she promised to come back for hospitality hour to say hello. She's excited to catch up with you." She grinned. "I believe she plans to quiz you on a bird she saw."

He laughed. "I'm always willing to share my knowledge of ornithology with others."

"That's nice to know."

"I'm hoping to get some time out on the lake," Ryan commented. "Do you still have your kayaks?"

"Yes, of course." Grace winced, wondering if she would be forced to cut the lock off the shed to get them. "Let me know when you'd like to use one. We've had a few storms recently, so I've already stored them in the shed for the season."

"I've got some business to take care of, so I won't have as much free time as I usually do while I'm here," Ryan said. "But I'm hoping to get Spencer out for at least one morning of fishing."

Grace's heart skipped a beat at the mention of Spencer Lewis. He was a retired intelligence analyst for the FBI and owned a small pecan farm nearby. Their warm friendship had slowly blossomed into a deeper relationship. After a few minor bumps in the road, Grace and Spencer were now dating. And Grace couldn't have been happier.

"If I remember right, you two didn't catch a single fish last year," she teased.

"No, but we told plenty of sea stories," he said.

Grace grinned. "I'm not surprised."

"How's your uncle doing?" Ryan asked. "I remember he wasn't feeling well last year when I visited."

She warmed at the kind inquiry. "Fortunately, he's back to his normal, healthy self."

"Good. If he's up to it, maybe he could join Spencer and me out on the lake when we go fishing."

"So you can tell more tall tales?" Grace joked.

Ryan laughed. "Yep, it's what men do best."

"I'll be sure to let Gus know you asked about him and extend the offer," she said. "And you're more than welcome to stop by their place. They would love to see you."

"I'll be sure to do that," he said. "I didn't want to barge in on them."

"Nonsense. They'd be delighted," Grace assured him. "Now let's get you checked in." She moved behind the reception desk and handed him a registration form. "As always, you're in the Wisteria Loft Suite."

But he didn't take the form. He was staring at something at the top of the stairs.

Melinda stood there. Her long, dark-blonde hair hung loose past her shoulders in soft waves, and she wore a lavender shirt and jeans.

Ryan continued to stand there, intently gazing at the other guest.

Grace smiled. Now this was an interesting development. In the years that Ryan had been coming to the inn since his beloved wife, Beth, had passed away, he'd never once given any female more than a cursory glance . . . until now.

Maybe Ryan was finally ready to move on.

Not that Grace planned to meddle in her guests' lives. No, that was Winnie's department. On the other hand, Ryan was more than a guest. He was a friend. It wasn't meddling to give a friend a little nudge along the path to happiness, was it?

Melinda descended the stairs and stopped. "I'm sorry. I didn't mean to interrupt."

"You're not," Ryan said.

"I thought I'd read on the back veranda," Melinda said, holding up her book, "as long as I won't be in anyone's way. Is that all right?"

"Of course," Grace said. "I'd like you to meet one of our other guests. Melinda Rainey, this is Ryan Scoville. He's visited us every year since we opened, and he's an ornithologist."

"That's birds, right?" Melinda asked.

"Yes, but it's only a hobby," Ryan answered. "I'm a cabinetmaker by trade."

"Oh, a man who is good with his hands and has a soft spot for our furry friends." Melinda gestured at Winston who sat at Ryan's feet.

Ryan smiled.

"Melinda's visiting us from Roswell," Grace told Ryan.

"Georgia, not the other one," Melinda added.

"I'm from Athens," Ryan said with a grin. "Georgia, not the other one."

Melinda laughed. "Well, I'll let the two of you get back to business. Ryan, it was a pleasure to meet you, and I'll see you during the hospitality hour. Grace, how do I get to the back veranda?"

Grace took a moment to give Melinda the inn's layout as well as the information on the trails by the lake.

After Melinda left, Grace gave Ryan a knowing smile. "She's a lovely woman, and Winston adores her. You know how good his character judgment is."

Ryan cleared his throat and stared down at the registration form for a moment. When he glanced up, his eyes were glassy.

"I'm sorry. What did I say?" Grace reached out and touched his arm. This was why she didn't like to meddle. She knew from firsthand experience that there was no time limit on grief, and she shouldn't have pushed even a little.

Ryan smiled, but it didn't reach his eyes. "Nothing. You did nothing wrong. I was startled because Melinda looks so much like Beth. If I didn't know better, I'd say Melinda was her sister."

Grace winced. Could she have been any more blind? "Now that you mention it, I guess there is a resemblance. I didn't see it at first, but I will say I was instantly drawn to Melinda and felt like I was chatting with an old friend when she arrived."

"They say everyone has a twin out there," Ryan said. "I think I just met Beth's."

With that comment, Grace squashed any and all plans to play matchmaker between her guests. She'd have to say something to Winnie too. Her aunt couldn't pass up a chance to play Cupid.

"Is this going to be weird for you?" Grace asked gently. "I mean, will this be too hard, seeing someone who reminds you of Beth?"

"No, I'll be fine," Ryan said, his voice cracking. He certainly didn't sound fine.

"I can check with The Tidewater and see if they have a room available," Grace suggested. "We'd hate to see you go, but your comfort is all that matters."

"Thanks for your concern," Ryan said. "It'll be interesting, but I'll be all right."

Grace wasn't normally in the business of sending guests away, especially not loyal, repeat customers like Ryan. But she had once been a grieving widow, and she knew the kind of pain Ryan was going through.

Of course, all of that had changed four months ago when her supposedly deceased husband had turned up on her doorstep.

Some days Grace still wasn't sure which was worse: being a widow or finding out your husband abandoned you and your son for a fresh start. Fortunately, she'd worked through most of that issue, and her relationship with Spencer was a source of joy and comfort in her life.

She watched Ryan carry his suitcase toward the stairs. Was it too much to hope that he might find a similar happiness someday?

4

Melinda

So far, Melinda had spent the first day of her trip vacationing rather than soul-searching. She'd walked the trail along the lakeshore, watched a couple of squirrels play tag, tried to guess the types of birds she saw, and read fifty-six pages in her book. But she was no closer to figuring out her life than she had been when she arrived.

Sooner or later, she would have to come up with a plan because she didn't want to spend her entire nest egg. It was supposed to take care of her in her golden years. She was pretty sure forty-five didn't even come close to golden—it was more a faded mint green.

Tomorrow, with a clear head and a good night's rest, she'd tackle the problem of deciding on a new career. If only she knew how and where to start. Numbers were her game, not psychology. Maybe she'd take one of those online personality tests or stop by the library and check out a book on midlife career changes.

But right now, Melinda was ready for hospitality hour. It would be nice to get to know her fellow guests over appetizers. As she stepped onto the back veranda, she nearly ran into the man she'd met earlier.

"You almost took me out along with the side table," Ryan said with a chuckle. "Do you always walk so purposefully?"

"I'm so sorry." Groaning inside, Melinda squeezed her eyes shut and wished for a do-over. "I'm a little preoccupied this evening." She grimaced. "Hopefully, I didn't leave any bruises or break any bones."

"No worries," he said, smiling. "I'm tougher than I look."

She laughed, suddenly a bit nervous.

"Would you care to join me for a glass of wine?" Ryan asked, his eyes kind. "Charlotte is an excellent chef, and there's a nice selection of snacks over here."

Melinda began to feel more at ease. "Both sound wonderful. Thank you."

He ushered her over to the buffet table and poured two glasses of wine.

Melinda filled her plate with a variety of appetizers, then followed him to a table.

Ryan handed her a glass of wine and sat down beside her.

When Melinda took a bite of a puff pastry, she groaned. Flavors exploded, tingling her taste buds. She savored the salty prosciutto and the touch of parmesan with a hint of Dijon mustard. Maybe she should enroll in a culinary school. She did love to cook.

"Wait until you try the shrimp puffs." He popped a bite into his mouth, and an expression of pure delight stole over his face. "I'm not much of a cook, but I've picked up a couple of Charlotte's cookbooks and everything I've made is wonderful. I even managed to impress my mom."

"I'll have to see if the local bookstore has any copies in stock, because this is absolutely divine," Melinda said. "I love cooking, but I'm nowhere near this level without a recipe to follow."

Ryan shook his head. "Don't worry about going to the bookstore. You can buy copies here at the inn. I'm planning to ask Charlotte to sign a copy so I can give it to my mom for Christmas."

"What a lovely idea." Melinda sipped her wine and settled in, trying to get comfortable under the weight of Ryan's gaze. "Are you close to your parents?"

"Yes, I am. I'm lucky to still have them both. What about you?"

"My parents live about two miles down the road and check in with me at least once a day," Melinda replied. "Every few days, my mom drops off leftovers because she always makes too much food. Once a week, we have a movie date." She grinned. "But sometimes we skip the movie and simply drink wine and chat."

Since Melinda had been laid off, her parents regularly invited her over for dinner or breakfast. Leftovers got dropped off more often too. Melinda figured it was her parents' way of helping to stretch her budget, even though they knew she didn't need the help.

"That's wonderful," Ryan said. "Are you an only child?"

"Sadly, yes. When I was five, I begged for a brother or a sister, but I got a puppy instead."

He laughed. "Sounds like a good trade-off."

"Do you have any siblings?" she asked.

"I've got an older brother and a younger sister," Ryan answered. "They're both married, and they have half a dozen kids between them. The holidays are loud and chaotic, but they're also fun and filled with laughter, a lot of teasing, and good old-fashioned sibling squabbling."

Melinda sensed an undercurrent of sadness to his words and wondered what was bothering him. She discreetly peeked at his ring finger. There was no wedding band, not even an indentation. She imagined it was difficult for Ryan to be the only unmarried sibling in a large family. If his parents were anything like hers, they wouldn't be satisfied until all their children were happily married with children of their own.

Her parents were great, but sometimes they took helpful to a new extreme, like when they'd signed her up for a dating website. Parents really had no idea what constituted embarrassment when it came to pictures or profiles. Or maybe they did. The jury was still out on that.

Either way, Melinda knew her mom and dad meant well. They wanted her to be happy, and their version of it included wedding bells and kids. Not that hers didn't too. If that was what fate had in store for her.

Once, a long time ago, she'd thought she'd met Mr. Right. But he'd turned out to be Mr. Wrong for her and Mr. Right for his coworker. Such a cliché. After that, Melinda had thrown herself into work, volunteering at her church and helping out at the town community center, where she filled boxes of food for those in need and tutored kids in math. She had loved her life until a couple of months ago.

As Melinda and Ryan continued to talk, she couldn't help but notice how he kept staring at her. At first, it was a little flattering. She wasn't vain by a long shot. She had a mirror after all, and enough people had commented over the years about how she was the spitting image of her mother, who was gorgeous. Not that Melinda agreed. Yes, there was a resemblance, but she had traces of her dad too, like his wide forehead and narrow chin. So, she doubted Ryan's constant gaze was a result of her blinding beauty, which made her concerned. Did she have something on her face? Cream cheese from the puffs? Lipstick on her nose? Raccoon eyes from her mascara?

While he talked about his passion for birds, Melinda rubbed the end of her nose and swiped a finger under her eyes. Just in case.

"Is everything okay?" Ryan asked.

"Yes," she said. "Why do you ask?"

"You're rubbing your face," he said, "and I was wondering if you were having an allergic reaction to something."

He was so calm about it that she laughed. If the roles were reversed and she thought he were having some sort of medical issue, she would have been a basket case. But Ryan remained cool and collected, like one of those suave gentlemen from days gone by. Melinda could easily see herself falling for him. But she wasn't in Magnolia Harbor for romance. She was here to clear her head and get some perspective on her life, not complicate it.

Before she could respond to his comment, an older woman approached.

Ryan introduced Winnie Bennett to Melinda and explained that she was the innkeepers' aunt, who helped out at the inn.

"How is your stay so far?" Winnie asked Melinda.

"It's wonderful. My room is absolutely gorgeous, and I love this social hour. It's such a nice touch."

"It's a great way for the guests to unwind and get to know each other," Winnie said. "And to sample Charlotte's incredible food."

"She's a terrific cook," Melinda agreed.

Winnie nodded, then addressed Ryan. "It's so good to see you again. Gus would have stopped over this evening, but he got busy with a train set he's building. You'll have to come by the house and say hello."

"I will," Ryan said. "Perhaps tomorrow after I've met with my client."

"Perfect," Winnie said. "I was planning to bake a loaf of pumpkin bread, along with beef and vegetable barley soup for lunch. I hope you'll join us."

"You don't have to ask me twice." Ryan rubbed his hands together and smiled.

"It sounds like good cooking runs in the family," Melinda remarked.

"I'd like to think so," Winnie said. She handed Melinda an old tin. "I wanted to give you this."

"For me?" Melinda asked, surprised. It was an odd gift.

"Yes, I think you might find it'll come in handy." Winnie excused herself to go mingle with the other guests.

"What did she give you?" Ryan asked.

"I don't know. Some kind of tin container. It's pretty beat-up, and most of the lettering has worn off." Melinda rubbed the top of it. She squinted and made out the words *mint tea*.

"Do you like antiques?" Ryan asked.

"Sure." Melinda slid the tin into her purse, then grinned at Ryan. "Is that another hobby of yours?"

"I recently started getting into it," he answered. "I'm hoping to stop by a few stores in the area. Maybe we could go together, if you're interested."

That sounded like a date. Warring emotions swirled inside Melinda. She was interested because Ryan was kind, funny, intriguing, and good-looking. But she was also cautious because she had other more important things to focus on.

"That would be fun," she said, "but can we play it by ear?"

"No problem," he said. "Part of my trip is related to business. Until I talk with the client, I'm not sure how my schedule will shape up yet. If we both find we have some free time and we're in the mood, we'll go. But if not, no worries."

"Are you always this easygoing?" Melinda asked, impressed with his response.

Ryan seemed to emit a peaceful, soothing energy. Maybe being around him was exactly what she needed, because for the first time in months, her stomach wasn't cramped up, her head didn't have that dull ache, and her neck and shoulder muscles weren't rock hard.

"Over the years, I've learned not to stress the stuff that's out of my hands." Ryan gazed across the veranda and spotted their hostess. "Can you excuse me? I need to talk to Grace."

"Of course."

After Ryan left, Melinda glanced around and noticed a younger woman sipping wine and talking to Winnie. The two women laughed, which in turn made everyone else smile.

A moment later, the woman locked eyes with Melinda, then rushed over and plopped down into Ryan's abandoned chair. "I have to tell you that it's so cute the way your husband gazes at you when you're not looking. It's like you're the only one in the room. I hope that's how my boyfriend, Chris, sees me."

Heat flushed over Melinda's cheeks. "He's not my husband. Actually, we just met today." She laughed and covered her face, trying to regain her composure. "Were you serious?"

"Absolutely," the woman said. "So, why don't you tell me all about yourself? Where are you from? What do you do? Do you have family here? What's your least favorite thing to eat? What's the craziest thing you've ever done?"

"How about we start off by introducing ourselves? I'm Melinda Faye Rainey, but my friends call me Melinda."

"I'm Tiffany Jackson, and I have a feeling we're going to be friends."

Melinda took a sip of her wine, liking Tiffany very much. "To answer your first question, I'm from Roswell—Georgia, not New Mexico."

"Really? Because your accent sounds more southwest to me." Tiffany giggled. "I'm actually right down the road from you in Atlanta."

"Small world."

"So what do you do?" Tiffany asked.

"I'm an accountant," Melinda said. "Or at least I was. I've been job hunting for several months, and I'm not sure what I am right now. If you ask me again at the end of the week, maybe I'll have a new answer for you. No, I don't have family here. I'm using my stay as a retreat to recharge my batteries and get some perspective."

"This seems like the ideal place to relax," Tiffany replied. "Did you see the view from our rooms? I'm sure Grace and Charlotte wouldn't mind if you took one of the chairs down and sat under that big old magnolia tree and read for the day."

"That's very tempting. Now, what were your other questions? Oh yes, least favorite food is marshmallows. Hate them. And we have to get to know each other better before I tell you the craziest thing I've ever done, but the scariest was giving my heart away."

Tiffany gasped. "I didn't realize you were married. I'm sorry for playing matchmaker between you and the other guest."

"I didn't say he kept my heart when I gave it away."

Tiffany reached out and placed her hand over Melinda's. "It was his loss. You're not still in mourning or anything, are you?"

Melinda laughed and shook her head. "I moved on a long time ago. Now, tell me what brings you to our little oasis."

"I'm here to meet my aunt," Tiffany answered.

"Wonderful. Will she be staying here at the inn with you?"

Tiffany clasped her hands and didn't respond.

"Wait a minute," Melinda said. "Do you mean meet as in you've never met your aunt before?"

Tiffany let out a shaky breath. "Yeah, exactly. I'm still trying to wrap my head around the fact that my mom had a sister. My mom never mentioned her once in thirty years, and I have no idea why."

"Can't you ask your mom?" Melinda asked gently.

"No, she passed away a couple of weeks ago," Tiffany said. "She only told me about her sister in a letter she left me with her last wishes. No explanation to the absence of her in our lives. My mom simply asked me to deliver a necklace to her sister and let her know that she was gone."

"What a shock for you," Melinda said. "When do you meet her?"

"Tomorrow." A lone tear slipped down Tiffany's cheek. "I can't believe I'm going to meet my aunt, who is a complete stranger to me."

"Do you want some company when you meet her?" Granted, Melinda was a complete stranger to Tiffany as well, but she felt an immediate connection to her and wanted to offer her support.

Tiffany wiped her cheek and gave Melinda a sad smile. "I should apologize. Here I am, crying all over you and dumping my baggage at your feet. I haven't had anyone to discuss this with, except my boyfriend. He tries to understand and be supportive, but he hasn't had much time to talk. He's in the service and getting ready to deploy. I know we just met, but it feels like I've known you forever."

"I get it," Melinda said. "No apology needed. My offer still stands, if you want it."

"Thank you for the kind offer and for listening, but I need to visit my aunt on my own." Tiffany took a sip of her wine and sat back. "How about we change the subject?"

"Sounds good," Melinda said. She heard voices and glanced across the room to see Ryan chatting with Winnie. It was obvious they were old friends given the easy laughter between them. Grace and Charlotte stopped by and added to their conversation.

If Melinda had to guess, she'd bet he was talking about birds since he was so animated. She didn't even realize how captivated she'd been by him until Tiffany nudged her shoe.

"We could go join them," Tiffany suggested with a grin.

"No, let them catch up," Melinda said, returning her full attention to Tiffany. "I'm sorry for being rude. Please tell me about yourself. What do you do? What don't I serve you at a dinner party?"

"You know the biggest things already," Tiffany said. "My boyfriend's in the Army, my mom died, and I'm meeting my mystery aunt. Besides that, I'm a software programmer. Yes, I was one of those geeks in school who was more comfortable with a computer than people. Oh, and I love animals. I hate shopping. I don't really cook a lot, but I eat pretty much anything and everything."

"Look at us," Melinda teased. "A couple of nerds. No wonder we hit it off. I've got a thing for numbers, and you've got a thing for tech. What kind of software programs do you work on?" *Please let them be programs I understand.* While Melinda was great with numbers, technology wasn't necessarily her friend, and she didn't want to come across as dated and ignorant.

"Mostly business software to help companies run more efficiently," Tiffany replied. "I've worked on all sorts, like the programs used by stores for scanning labels so cashiers don't have to manually enter every item. My last project was an inventory tracking program, and I was supposed to start on a new accounting program, but that was when my mom got sick."

Melinda's wine turned to vinegar in her stomach, and she felt ill. She couldn't discuss work anymore. She needed some space. "I'm so sorry, but suddenly I'm not feeling well. Probably too much wine and not enough food combined with a long day. I think I'm going to take a walk down by the lake. Maybe that will help."

"I'll bet it was all my talking," Tiffany commented. "My mom always said I was a chatterbox."

"Nonsense," Melinda said. "We'll chat again later."

Once Melinda was out on the lawn, she followed the path down to the lake and the inn's dock, where she found a couple of Adirondack chairs. She remained standing as she gazed at the water.

Resentment toward Tiffany ate away her. Even though she knew it was wrong, she couldn't help it. She'd worked hard for her employer for so many years only to be replaced by a computer, by a software program that was supposed to complete the work in half the time. Tiffany probably believed she was making businesses more efficient, but she didn't realize she was destroying people's livelihoods.

What had started off as a warm September day had become a cool autumn evening, with the breeze gently blowing off the lake. The water softly lapped at the shore. The anger that had consumed her moments ago washed away as Melinda let the night surround and comfort her in a peaceful blanket.

If I don't let go of these negative emotions, I'm never going to move forward, she thought.

Melinda was tired of being stuck in the past. It was time to move on. While it hadn't seemed like it at first, losing her job was a blessing in disguise, a second chance to do something amazing with her life.

But the question remained: What else was she qualified to do?

She didn't have a college degree. Accounting had been her only job, and going back to school at forty-five sounded even more daunting than finding a new career.

Dropping into one of the chairs, Melinda started to make a plan for the next day. She'd swing by the library for a few books and do an Internet search on jobs that didn't require college degrees. Maybe she'd spot one she'd missed on her previous searches.

"Feeling any better?" asked a soft voice behind her.

Melinda jumped and spun around to see Ryan standing there. "Much. But how did you know?"

"I saw you leave and asked Tiffany if everything was okay," he answered. "She mentioned you weren't feeling well."

Melinda nodded, touched that he had asked about her.

"I made a dinner reservation at The Tidewater on the other side of the lake," Ryan said. "Would you like to join me?"

She hesitated. A date? She wanted to move forward in her career, but now was not the time for a romance.

"We could ask Tiffany to come along too, if you'd like," he added.

When Ryan put it like that, it was no longer a date, so Melinda couldn't see any reason to say no. Smiling, she stood up. "Let's go. I'm starving."

5

Tiffany

Tiffany sighed as she set her brush down and glanced into the bathroom mirror. Her frizzy hair was as good as it was going to get with the humidity.

Now to choose the perfect outfit. Something that bolstered her confidence but was casual and comfortable. If there was such a thing. Mentally she discarded her favorite blue jeans, the black slacks, and the dark-blue dress she'd brought. The first was too casual, the second pinched at the waist, and the last would look like she was headed to a business meeting—or a funeral. Not the first impression she'd hoped to make with her aunt.

Surely Tiffany had packed something that would work. But she'd been so nervous about coming here that she hadn't paid much attention. She'd simply grabbed clothes and tossed them into her suitcase before she could lose her nerve and cancel the trip.

When Tiffany walked out of the bathroom, she stopped in her tracks. The room was a disaster. Her purse rested on the floor near the edge of the bed with the contents scattered. Clothes were strewn across the bed, and she didn't even remember throwing them before she took a shower. Then again, she'd been a little preoccupied.

A terrible thought hit her. Had someone been inside her suite? For good measure, Tiffany checked the doors leading to the hall and the veranda. Both were locked. The window was open, but it had a screen in place. There was no way anyone could have climbed in through that window. Besides, it would have been much easier to enter the room through the French doors off the veranda. The only thing she did notice was a medium-sized tear in the screen.

Unless her room had been invaded by Lilliputians, she was safe—just messy and forgetful.

Tiffany gathered the contents of her purse and put them back, then set the bag on the dresser, making sure it was away from the edge so it wouldn't slide off again.

Then she turned her attention to the clothes on her bed. As she sorted through them, she groaned. Why couldn't she find anything appropriate to wear? It wasn't as if she dressed like a slob. Her clothes weren't stained or full of holes.

"Why does it even matter?" she grumbled to no one.

Tiffany had never really stressed about first impressions before, so this felt weird and out of character for her. She didn't lack self-esteem. Tiffany knew she was a good person, reasonably intelligent, and a little witty. Most of the time, she could talk to anyone. So why was she stressing now?

Because this wasn't a stranger she was meeting. It was her aunt. Her flesh and blood. Her mother's sister. A woman who should have loved Tiffany and her mother unconditionally, but for some unknown reason had vacated their lives before Tiffany was even born. This woman was her last living relative, and Tiffany thought it was important to get to know her because she didn't want to be alone. But it was more than that. Tiffany didn't want to embarrass her parents.

Today was the day Tiffany would solve the mystery behind whatever rift had separated the sisters and begin the process of bringing her family back together. Granted, it was only the two of them now, and Tiffany hadn't been involved in whatever the issue was, but she hoped her aunt didn't extend the grudge to her.

Finally, she settled on a pair of dark jeans and a lightweight, cotton shirt in lemon yellow to brighten her mood.

As she dressed and hung up the rest of her clothes, she tried to remember what her mother's letter had said about her aunt Laura. Not much. Her mother wanted Tiffany to break the news of her passing to Laura and give her the necklace. It was a gold arrow with an amethyst. Her mom hadn't mentioned what was special about the necklace or why she wanted her sister to have it.

Tiffany had asked her mother about the necklace many times while growing up. She'd wondered where it had come from and why she never took it off. But Tiffany's mom had always refused to talk about it. All these years, Tiffany had assumed the necklace had been a gift from her grandfather, but now she wasn't so sure.

Before she could think too much more on the subject, her cell phone rang. She checked the screen and smiled. It was Chris.

"Did you meet her?" he asked. "How did it go?"

"Not yet," Tiffany said. "I'm heading over to her house in a few minutes. I'm so nervous. What if she won't talk to me?"

"Don't be nervous," Chris urged. "Everyone likes you. She'll love you, just like I do."

"I hope you're right."

"Of course I am," he said. "So when are you coming home?"

"It depends on how today goes. If it's bad, then I'll leave tomorrow. If it's good, I'll stay until the end of the week. Why? What's going on?"

"I got my orders in," Chris answered. "My deployment was moved up. I'm leaving in a month, and I want to spend as much time as I can with you before I go."

"That's horrible," Tiffany said, her spirits sinking. "I was hoping we'd get at least Thanksgiving together."

"Me too. I'm sorry, but you know how it is."

"Yeah, I know. I'll be home soon. Work is bugging me to come back too."

"That's good, right?"

"I'm not sure," Tiffany admitted. "Sitting in an office all day with no one to talk to is kind of depressing. Truthfully, I haven't really missed it."

"Then it's time to find something else that makes you happier," Chris suggested.

"Like what?" Tiffany asked.

"I have no idea," he said. "What do you want to do?"

"I'll have to think about it, and I'll let you know how today goes. Love you."

"Love you too. Good luck."

After disconnecting the call, Tiffany decided it was going to be a good day after all. Even if her aunt didn't want anything to do with her, she wouldn't be alone—she had Chris. Maybe after this next deployment they'd talk about making the relationship more permanent. Both had hinted at a future together. She'd even suspected that Chris was going to propose this past summer on their second anniversary, but then her mom had gotten gravely ill.

For the past couple of months, all Tiffany's time and energy had gone into caring for her mother. It was a miracle that Chris had stuck with her and a testament to what a great guy he really was. He'd given up his free time to help Tiffany by mowing the lawn, cooking dinner, and sitting with her mother while she ran to the store.

All the while, her mom had rambled about things that made no sense. It was only after Tiffany read the letter that she realized her mom had been trying to talk about her sister, but the medications she'd been taking had jumbled her words.

Tiffany would be sure to tell her aunt that she was the person her mother had thought of day in and day out as the end neared.

Tucking her phone into her purse, she scanned the room to confirm that she'd picked up her mess. She hated to be a rude and untidy guest. When her gaze landed on the torn screen, she made a mental note to tell Grace or Charlotte.

It was still early, so Tiffany headed downstairs for breakfast. She went to the dining room and took in the offerings. First things first . . . caffeine. She filled a cup with hot water and studied the assorted tea bags in the basket. Today called for a clear head, so she picked Earl Grey and added a good dose of honey.

Tiffany set her cup down on the table, then filled a plate with quiche, fresh fruit, and a maple-pecan scone.

Melinda entered the room and greeted her warmly. "Do you mind if I join you for breakfast?"

"Please do," Tiffany said as she took a seat.

Melinda grabbed a plate and helped herself to breakfast and a cup of coffee. She sat down across from Tiffany. "I hope I didn't wake you up this morning. I'm afraid I couldn't sleep, so I sat out on the veranda reading."

"Did you?" Tiffany asked. "I was out for the count."

"How are you feeling about seeing your aunt today?" Melinda peered at her over the rim of her coffee cup. "My offer to go with you still stands, if you change your mind."

"That's sweet, but I'm good." Tiffany thought about it for a moment. Was she really? She was nervous, but there was nothing to be done about that. Until she met Laura Devereux, she was going to be a heap of jumbled nerves, but overall, she'd be fine. "To be honest, I was a wreck this morning. I must have tossed every item of clothing I brought with me all over my room—twice—in an attempt to find the right outfit."

"Yellow is a lovely color on you," Melinda assured her. "What time are you meeting your aunt?"

Tiffany focused on cutting her quiche into tiny pieces. "Well, I didn't tell her that I'm coming. So, I hope she's home when I arrive."

Melinda gaped at her with her coffee cup suspended in midair. "Do you mean you came to town without checking to see if she'd be home first?"

Tiffany nodded.

"What if she's on vacation?" Melinda asked. "Or at work? What if she moved, and some strange and scary people live in her house now? You definitely shouldn't go alone."

All those thoughts and more had already gone through Tiffany's brain. But in the end, she was afraid to give her aunt advance notice of her arrival in case Laura used it as an excuse to avoid her.

"Trust me," Tiffany said. "I've already considered all that. The last suggestion has cost me more than a few hours' sleep, which is why I'm going during the day. I'm also leaving the address with you and Grace and Charlotte in case I don't return. If my aunt's not at home, I'll check with a neighbor to find out when she'll be back."

Melinda bit her bottom lip. "I could sit in the car. That way if something or someone looks dangerous, I could call for help instead of us waiting hours to make sure you return."

Tiffany got the feeling that the other woman's offer had more behind it than assuring her safety, not that she doubted Melinda's sincerity. "Is everything okay? I mean, are you trying to avoid someone or something by coming with me? Or did you have a bad experience and this is giving you flashbacks?"

"Oh goodness, no." Melinda set down her cup with a clatter. "I'm so sorry. I realize how weird that sounded. No, there's no trauma in my past. I hear so much on the news that I just overreacted."

"Are you sure?" Tiffany persisted.

"Honestly, I am trying to avoid my own life issues. Please ignore me." Melinda picked up her scone and broke it in half. "But promise that you'll text me when you get there and when you leave. Okay?"

"I can do that," Tiffany said.

After they exchanged numbers, Tiffany grinned. "Now tell me about your conversation with Ryan after I left last night."

Dinner had been relaxing, fun, and delicious as she got to know both Melinda and Ryan. However, Tiffany had spent most of the evening watching the two of them connect over the Brie, commiserate over their mutual dislike of brussels sprouts, and blush at each other's compliments. While Tiffany had enjoyed the meal, it was clear to her that her dining companions were meant for each other, which was why she'd hurried to her suite as soon as they returned to the inn.

"There's nothing to tell," Melinda said. "He had an appointment early this morning, so he already left."

"I'm not talking about this morning," Tiffany explained. "I was asking about last night. It was a beautiful evening for a stroll along the lakeshore. Such a missed opportunity." She laughed. "Sorry, but I thought you two had an amazing connection."

"I take it you're a hopeless romantic," Melinda said.

"A hopeful romantic," Tiffany corrected her.

Charlotte walked into the dining room with a fresh pot of coffee. "Good morning. Is there anything else I can get for either of you?"

"No, breakfast was perfect. I especially love the scones." Tiffany patted her stomach and smiled. "Maybe a little too much. I might need to go explore those walking trails."

"Music to my ears," Charlotte said. "If there's anything Grace or I can do to make your stay more enjoyable, please don't hesitate to tell us."

"Oh, I noticed there's a tear in my window screen," Tiffany said.

"Thanks for letting me know," Charlotte said. "We'll get it fixed."

"Actually, there is something else," Tiffany said, then glanced at Melinda. "Do you know when Ryan will be back?"

Charlotte smiled. "Normally, we don't give out that kind of information about our guests. I'm sure you understand that discretion and privacy are highly valued here at the inn."

Tiffany did understand, but she couldn't deny that she was disappointed. She had only wanted to help out Melinda because she knew that her new friend would never ask.

Charlotte set the coffeepot on the table. "By the way, I'm making my crab-stuffed mushrooms for hospitality hour. No one's allergic to shellfish, are they?"

"Not me," Tiffany said.

"Me either," Melinda said. "They sound wonderful."

"Oh good," Charlotte responded. "They're a favorite of Ryan's. I don't think he's ever missed an opportunity to have them." She winked and left the two alone.

Both women burst out laughing.

"Now that was discreet," Melinda said.

"But astute," Tiffany said. "And it proves that I'm not the only one who noticed the spark between you and Ryan."

"Shouldn't you be focused on your meeting with your aunt?" Melinda's blush and the slight lift of her lips suggested that Tiffany wasn't wrong in her assessment of the woman's interest in the other guest.

"Probably, but this is so much more fun," Tiffany said. Just thinking about her aunt flipped her stomach upside down.

Melinda sighed. "It might be more fun, but it's pointless. I'm not on vacation for a romance. I'm here to get my head on straight and my life sorted out."

"But that's exactly it," Tiffany said. "Maybe you need a break from life."

"What does that even mean?"

"For the past several months, you've been neck-deep in this turmoil," Tiffany reminded her. "You've been searching for a job and applying for countless positions. I'll bet you've taken no time to indulge yourself or take care of your mental health. Maybe if you allowed yourself a break and engaged in a little romance, you'd go home with a new outlook on life." She grinned. "And who knows what else?"

Melinda sat back, tapping her cup. "You might have a point."

Before Tiffany could say anything else, Winston trotted into the room, followed by Grace. The little dog ran first to Melinda, who gave him a snuggle and scratched his ears. Then he jumped down and raced over to Tiffany.

"Good morning to you too, Winston," Tiffany said.

Winston barked and hopped onto her lap.

Simply being around the dog lifted everyone's mood, especially hers. Maybe after Tiffany got settled in at work, she'd visit the local humane society and find a dog of her own. A pet who would love her unconditionally and keep her company during the long months while her boyfriend was deployed.

Then Tiffany remembered that she would have her mom's dog, Daisy, to love. The thought was like getting hit in the gut, taking her breath away. She loved Daisy, but of course she'd rather have her mom.

"Winston has been whining to say hello," Grace told them as she checked the breakfast buffet. "How is everything this morning? Did you both sleep well?"

Tiffany and Melinda praised Charlotte's cooking and raved about their beds, their rooms, and the inn in general.

"That's good to hear," Grace said, but she sounded distracted as she scanned the room.

"Are you still searching for your key?" Melinda asked.

Grace jumped, almost as if she had forgotten they were sitting there. "Yes, I am, and I'm also trying to find my thimble. Please forgive me. I'm not usually so scattered and rude."

"You're neither," Melinda assured her. "Maybe we can help keep an eye out for both items. In the meantime, I'm going to explore downtown Magnolia Harbor."

"If you want some exercise, we have bicycles that you can borrow," Grace offered. "It's a lovely day for a ride."

"That would be nice," Melinda said. "It's been a long time since I've been on a bike."

"I went for an early morning ride and left the bike in the front yard," Grace said. "It's leaning against a tree."

"Thanks," Melinda said, then turned to Tiffany. "Please don't forget to text me when you arrive at your aunt's. I'll feel much better knowing when you get there and leave."

"Will do, ma'am." Tiffany mock-saluted her new friend and grinned.

"I'll see you both later." Melinda smiled at Tiffany and left.

"I asked Charlotte and Winnie if they know Laura Devereux," Grace said.

Tiffany snuggled with Winston as she waited to hear Grace's answer and any details she could provide. If only someone would say whether her aunt was a good person or not, at least she'd have some kind of idea of what to expect. "Any luck?"

"I'm afraid not." Grace collected the empty dishes and smiled. "But I'm sure your reunion will be everything you're hoping for."

"From your lips to God's ears." Tiffany gently set Winston on the floor, then rose and dusted the crumbs off her jeans.

It was time to grant her mother's dying wish. She prayed she wouldn't regret it.

6

Melinda

Melinda found the bicycle right where Grace said it would be, leaning against a tree in the front yard.

Melinda appreciated Grace's kind offer to borrow her bike, but she couldn't help but feel a bit wary. It was true when she'd told Grace and Tiffany that she hadn't been on a bicycle in a long time. But how hard could it be? She had learned how to ride a bike when she was a kid, so she couldn't have forgotten.

Right. Except she wasn't an elephant. She forgot things.

Melinda hoped she wouldn't end up in the emergency room with a dislocated elbow like that time when she was five. Granted, she'd been hotdogging and may or may not have been trying her hand at stunts far beyond her skill level. Those were the good old days when she'd been carefree and daring, attempting anything that caught her attention, much to her mother's dismay.

These days, Melinda lived a cautious life, much to her own dismay.

She carefully got on the bicycle and began pedaling. As she navigated the wobbling bike down the driveway and along Lake Haven Road to town, she thought about the past twenty-four hours. She'd gone on vacation while unemployed. That wasn't exactly practical or cautious. Surprisingly, she'd already made a friend, even though Tiffany was responsible for putting real people out of work. And she'd met someone who'd made her think of something other than numbers for once.

Whether a relationship with Ryan might go anywhere or not remained unclear.

A part of her wanted to throw her long-held caution to the wind and take Tiffany's advice in regards to Ryan: have a vacation romance and take a break from life.

But after leading a cautious life for so many years, it was a hard habit to break. Even if Melinda wanted to be careless and carefree, it didn't mean Ryan was interested in anything more than a friendly face to converse with over canapés and crème brûlée.

No, her focus needed to be on figuring out her life. Technically, there was no big hurry to find a new job. Over the years, she'd invested wisely and built a substantial nest egg. But that cushion was to make her golden years comfortable. Besides, she wanted to work.

It was wonderful and relaxing to take vacations like this, but Melinda needed something more in her life to keep her busy. It would be different if she'd had a family to tend. But it was just her. She didn't even have a dog or a cat.

As she turned onto Main Street in town, a few people she didn't know waved to her, and she waved back. She rode around for a while, scanning the charming shops, including Spool & Thread, The Book Cottage, Miss Millie's, and the Dragonfly Coffee Shop.

Then she ventured into the nearby residential area and admired the pretty houses with their unique styles and flourishes, beautiful flower gardens in an array of colors, and glorious fountains. Most of the homes were white and trimmed in either blue or red, but every now and then she saw a blue or a yellow one. Melinda absolutely loved the pink-and-purple Victorian on one of the corners. It made her wonder about the occupants. She was certain that they didn't lead a cautious life.

Melinda returned to Main Street and hopped off the bike. After her ride, she was hot and thirsty, so she walked her bike to the Dragonfly Coffee Shop and propped it up by the door. The outside tables were surprisingly empty.

When Melinda entered the coffee shop, she eyed the empty tables. Maybe she should find another café. An empty coffee shop didn't bode well for the quality of their food and drinks.

A younger woman in her twenties, with her long, dark hair pulled into a ponytail, glanced up from where she'd been working on something at the counter. "Welcome to the Dragonfly. What can I get for you?"

"Oh, I wasn't sure if you were open yet or not," Melinda said, trying to cover up her thoughts of running out the door.

The woman grinned. "We're experiencing an unusual lull in business, so I'm all yours."

Melinda approached the counter and glanced down, surprised to see a drawing instead of inventory that she'd assumed the woman to be working on. It was a simple pencil drawing of a magnolia tree. "That's lovely."

"Thank you. Normally, I don't sketch while I'm working, but I was inspired."

"What were you inspired by?" Melinda asked as she peered out the window. The magnolia trees outside had already bloomed for the season, but the tree in the drawing was in full bloom.

"I don't know, but some of our best ideas hit out of the blue, right?"

"I guess," Melinda said. "Truthfully, I'm not the creative type. I'm more of a numbers person."

"Ah, numbers." She laughed. "My nemesis."

Melinda scanned the menu and ordered an iced vanilla latte and an apple-cranberry fritter. She'd burned more than enough calories on her bike ride to justify the treat.

The woman handed Melinda the pastry, then went to work on her drink order. "I haven't seen you in here before. Are you new in town or passing through?"

Melinda picked at the edge of her fritter, breaking off a small bite as her stomach growled. It seemed that she'd worked up more of an appetite than she'd thought. "I'm a guest at the Magnolia Harbor Inn. Melinda Faye Rainey."

"Nice to meet you. I'm Angel Diaz. Artist and barista extraordinaire." She smiled. "Lucky you. The Magnolia Harbor Inn is a wonderful place, and Grace and Charlotte are the best."

"That they are."

"I'm surprised you have room for that pastry after Charlotte's breakfast," Angel remarked. "She's an amazing cook."

Melinda took another bite of her snack. "To be honest, I thought after breakfast I'd be full until dinner tonight, but it was worth every calorie."

"What did she make this morning?" Angel asked.

"Maple-pecan scones that melted in my mouth," Melinda answered. "I ate three of them."

"Those sound divine. I'll have to get the recipe from Charlotte and see if she minds if we serve them here. A lot of our goodies are actually her recipes, including that fritter. So, enjoy."

"Oh, I am," Melinda said. "I biked into town and didn't realize how hungry it would make me."

"Well, it's the perfect day for that," Angel said. "There are a few trails along the lake that you can take too. I highly recommend them. Grace and Charlotte also have kayaks you can borrow, if you feel like getting out on the water."

"Sounds nice," Melinda said. "Thanks for the tips."

Angel scrawled her signature at the bottom of the drawing, then handed it to Melinda with her coffee. "A remembrance of your trip to Magnolia Harbor."

"Thank you," Melinda said. "I wish I could draw, but that wasn't a gift I was graced with. I'm all left brain. Give me a good sudoku puzzle, and I'm happy. It's all logic. But if I attempt to create something, it'll look like a toddler did it."

Angel laughed as she came around the counter with a dish towel in her hand and started wiping down the already clean tables. "I'm betting you're not that bad. Besides, not being traditionally 'good' at something doesn't mean you can't enjoy doing it. You probably haven't found the right medium for your creative outlet. Have you tried knitting or quilting?"

"I can't say that I have." Melinda took a seat at a table by the window, careful not to spill any crumbs. "Do you do those as well?"

Angel nodded. "Actually, I belong to a quilting group in town, and we meet at six every Tuesday evening at Spool & Thread. Winnie Bennett is also a member. You're welcome to join us."

"I met Winnie last night," Melinda said. "She's a nice lady, but she seems a bit strange."

Angel smiled. "Aren't we all a bit strange, though?"

"Yes, I guess you're right." Melinda returned the smile. "I appreciate the invitation. I'll think about popping in."

Before disappearing through a door behind the counter, Angel told her to ring the bell if she needed anything. She'd be in the back baking a batch of muffins before the afternoon crowd arrived.

Melinda settled in with her fritter and coffee. She pulled out her phone, intent on reading an e-book, when an e-mail notification popped up. With her heart in her throat, she opened her mail account. Right before leaving on the trip, she'd sent out another round of résumés in the hopes one of them would spark an interview.

First, she deleted the junk. Some would call what she was doing stalling, but she called it being efficient. Soon there was only one e-mail left. It was from a major accounting firm in her hometown.

Melinda swallowed the fritter that had suddenly become a lump in her throat and said a little prayer. Then she clicked on the message and read it. Her heart plummeted.

Rejection number eighty-nine.

The tears didn't even come anymore. They'd stopped somewhere around rejection number twenty-seven. Now it was a sad acceptance. No one wanted to hire her. They all assured her that her résumé was great and she would be an asset to any company, but they weren't hiring an accountant. With all the automation, there wasn't the need for as many people as there used to be.

A bluebird landed on a chair outside her window and chirped at her. It was as if he were asking, "Well, what now?"

Melinda didn't know. Honestly, she wasn't even sure if the rejection was a blessing or a disappointment. It was such a nice day, and she'd enjoyed her ride tremendously, so much that she'd planned to find the bike trails Angel had mentioned. If she had a job right now, she'd be cooped up inside an office. Who would want to be working on a day like today?

Of course, that had been her life for more than twenty-five years, but wasn't that long enough? Wasn't it time for a change? Her mother certainly thought so. She'd been advising Melinda for the past couple of years to find a new job, something that would make her feel fulfilled at the end of the day. The funny thing was, Melinda had believed she'd been fulfilled in her position until she'd been let go. Sure, it had hurt to be fired, but she was surprised to realize it had also been a relief.

Now Melinda no longer had to get up at five in the morning and work until ten during tax season. She had more time to see her parents and work at the community center.

And she had the opportunity to get outside and walk. No artificial lights, no artificial plants, no recycled air. She loved being outdoors.

"Hey, that's it," Melinda said. "Maybe I should become a gardener."

"Did you say something?" Angel had reappeared at the counter, transferring cookies to a cute bear-shaped jar on the counter.

"Sorry," Melinda said, embarrassed. "I was talking to myself. By the way, those cookies smell wonderful."

"Thanks," Angel said. "Chocolate chip with dried cherries and sunflower seeds. Would you like one? They're still warm."

Temptation urged her to say yes, but her waistband suggested otherwise. "Thank you, but I'll pass for now. Maybe tomorrow."

The door opened, and two women walked inside the shop.

Angel set the pan of cookies down and greeted the new arrivals.

Melinda mulled over the idea of gardening. On the plus side, she'd have the chance to work outside. She would breathe in fresh air daily, get some exercise, and create something that would give back to the community. On the negative side, she had a serious black thumb. She'd even killed her air plant, and everyone said that was impossible.

As Melinda watched Angel chat with the women at the counter, another idea struck her. She could open her own coffee shop. Roswell was sorely lacking in good old-fashioned cafés. There were a couple of chain coffee shops, but what the town needed was a neighborhood one. Melinda could serve cookies, muffins, soups, and sandwiches. Maybe even learn to make scones and quiche. And she'd let people sit and read or use their computers for however long they wanted. It would be a welcoming place for people to gather and socialize.

Oh, but wait. That meant getting up really early to bake. Melinda hated waking up when it was dark outside, and she was horrible about going to sleep when it was light out, which meant she'd get no sleep during the summer.

Okay, gardening and opening a coffee shop were both out.

What did a numbers gal do when she couldn't crunch numbers anymore?

Disgusted with her lack of progress and inability to sit still, Melinda set her empty glass in the dish tray at the end of the counter and threw her trash away. She waved to Angel, who was busy with a few more customers who had entered while Melinda had been lost in her thoughts.

Outside, she wheeled the bike out to the street and tried to decide where to go next. It seemed like that question was the only thing on her mind lately.

"Melinda!" someone called out.

She turned to see Ryan crossing the street toward her.

A slow smile tugged at her lips until she gave up the fight and smiled warmly in his direction. Ryan was handsome in a gray suit with a light-blue shirt and a striped tie. He was obviously still dressed for his earlier business meeting.

"How did your meeting go?" Melinda popped the bike back onto the sidewalk and wheeled it out of the other pedestrians' way.

"It went great," Ryan answered. "My client was really impressed with my bid and the suggestions I'd sent for the order. I'll need to go back a few more times this week for measurements and to work out the last-minute details, but I'm glad to say I got the job."

"That's wonderful," Melinda said. "What exactly will you be doing?"

"Designing and making custom cabinets for the kitchen and three bathrooms," he said. "Plus, his workshop where he produces his own wine."

Excitement radiated from him and wrapped around Melinda. Unable to resist, she reached out and patted his arm. "That's fabulous. It sounds like it will keep you busy for a while too."

"It'll take me about six months to complete all the work," he said. "If there are any changes or additions, it'll take even longer."

"Does that mean you'll be spending more time in Magnolia Harbor?" she asked.

"I probably won't need to return until we install the new cabinets." Ryan stuck his hands into his pant pockets. "But enough about work. How has your day been going?"

"Relaxing," Melinda said. "Grace lent me her bike, and I tooled around town before stopping in at the Dragonfly for a coffee and a bite to eat. I'm on my way back to the inn now. I heard there are some trails along the lake, and I thought I'd go explore some more."

Should Melinda ask him to join her? Or if he didn't want to bike, she could suggest something else like kayaking or bird-watching. She'd never actually asked a guy out before, which sounded kind of silly.

"That sounds great," Ryan commented. "If I didn't have a few things to finish, I would ask if you wanted some company."

Melinda realized that she was more disappointed about Ryan not being able to join her than she was about the job rejection. "Maybe another time?"

"I'm glad you said that."

"Oh?" Melinda asked.

He grinned as color flooded his cheeks.

She thought his blush was adorable. But wait, had she taken his comment wrong? He was probably blushing because she'd made him feel awkward.

"I was hoping you might join me for dinner tonight," Ryan said. "Turner's Lakeside Grill has wonderful steaks and seafood."

Melinda hesitated. She hadn't come here for a romance, and she needed to focus on the problem at hand—her lack of employment. But maybe Tiffany was right. A break from her worries might be exactly what she needed.

Of course, it took two to tango. She had to be imagining stars when there were only plain old lights shining in her eyes. Ryan likely just didn't want to eat alone. Then again, after their dinner last night and how well they'd connected, she questioned that. For the first time in a long time, she hoped that someone was interested in her.

Melinda smiled. "Dinner sounds great."

Tiffany

As Tiffany drove along the rural road, seeing nothing but open fields and trees for several miles between one house and the next, her imagination of serial killers kicked into overdrive.

She shook off her ridiculous thoughts when she arrived at her destination. The small log house was charming, but it wasn't quite what Tiffany had expected. Given that the woman who lived here was her mother's sister, Tiffany had anticipated a similar taste, only to be proven completely wrong. Her mom had loved exploring new places—she never would have moved so far from home or into the country.

It wasn't only the remote location that made Tiffany wonder about her aunt but the house itself. Her mom, while not materialistic, had been into creature comforts and modern technology. Tiffany wouldn't be surprised to see a pump handle for a well somewhere on the property next to the house.

Though the house could be described as rustic, the grounds were simply breathtaking. Flowers lined the house. More flowers overflowed in pots hanging from the porch and spilled out of barrels placed strategically around the yard. She imagined the view was a riot of color in the spring. Today it was gold, orange, and red from the mums. Off to the side sat a fountain with a stone bench perfectly situated to enjoy the morning sun and shade from the afternoon heat. Beyond the fountain was an arbor with the weathered vines of a clematis. All were a bit overgrown and wild yet still restricted to their allotted spaces. Contained chaos.

It was so unlike her mom, who had always been neat, precise, and controlled. The contrast between the two women's lifestyles was interesting, but it wasn't the reason why Tiffany was here. Excitement at meeting her long-lost aunt skittered over Tiffany's nerves. She breathed in deeply, then exhaled slowly.

Maybe she should come back tomorrow or send a letter asking her aunt to meet her somewhere in town. She could return to the inn and sit under that glorious weeping willow and lose herself in a book for a few hours. When was the last time she'd allowed herself to relax like that? It had been way too long.

But no, she'd journeyed all the way to South Carolina to grant her mother her dying wish.

Needing some reinforcement, Tiffany texted Chris. *I'm here, but I'm afraid to get out of the car. I should have waited for you to get leave.*

A few moments later, Chris responded. *I'm sorry I'm not there for you, but you've got this. After everything you've gone through, this will be a cakewalk.*

She huffed out a laugh, glad he had so much faith in her and wishing she had it in herself.

Tiffany almost forgot that she'd promised to text Melinda. She sent her new friend a short message to assure her that she had arrived safely.

"Okay, it's now or never," Tiffany said out loud. Steeling her nerves, she stepped out of the car. As she reached down for her purse, a familiar voice—so cherished and missed—called out to her.

"I thought you might be planning to sit out there in your car all day. If you're selling something, I'm probably not buying, but I'll listen to your spiel."

Tiffany blinked back tears. Even though her mom and aunt had completely different styles, their welcoming nature was the same.

She closed the car door, turned around, and froze. She smiled as a weight lifted from her shoulders and sadness lifted from her heart. "Mom?" she whispered.

Had it all been a terrible nightmare? Had Tiffany dreamed weeks of driving her mother to chemotherapy and radiation treatment, tending to her when she was too weak to get out of bed, and watching as her hair fell out by the handfuls?

No, Tiffany hadn't dreamed her mother taking her last breath while lying in her bed, holding her daughter's hand. That had been a real-life nightmare.

Reality crashed into her like a tsunami. This woman wasn't her mother. It was her mother's identical twin.

"Are you okay?" Laura Devereux asked.

Tiffany tried to answer, but as the pain wrapped around her heart and squeezed, she stumbled. She caught herself on the front fender. All she could do was shake her head.

She couldn't believe that her mother hadn't warned her about Laura. Why hadn't her mom realized that coming face-to-face with her spitting image would be a shock for her daughter? How could she have not known how heartbreaking it would be for Tiffany to see her face on another living person when she was gone forever?

Tiffany dropped her gaze. It simply hurt too much to see the one person she missed the most and know it wasn't her.

Meeting her long-lost aunt was one thing, but staring at her mother's face was overwhelming. It asked too much of her. How could Tiffany be strong now when she had already used up all her strength these last few months caring for her mom? Tiffany had been helpless to stop the inevitable, so seeing her mother's face on another person was a cruel reminder of how she'd failed.

Tiffany couldn't do this. She decided to return to the inn and mail the necklace to her aunt with a note. Whirling around, she reached her car door and fumbled for the handle. "I can't do it," she sobbed.

"Can't do what?" Her aunt hurried over to her, resting a warm hand on her arm. "You're in no shape to drive. Come up to the porch and sit down. I'll get you something cold to drink, and you can let it all out. You'll feel better."

Tiffany let her aunt usher her to the porch. She sat on a wicker rocker, and all the pain and grief she'd been holding in for the past two weeks flooded out. Vaguely she registered a door opening and closing, then repeating a few seconds later. With blurred vision and shaking hands, she accepted a cold glass of sweet tea, and somewhere in the back of her brain she knew Laura sat in the other rocker. But Tiffany said nothing. She simply let the tears fall.

After a while, the well ran dry, leaving her emotionally and physically drained. Tiffany glanced down to find a tissue in her hand and the box at her side. She used a tissue to wipe her face. Thank goodness she was wearing waterproof mascara, but she still looked like a mess, sitting there and wailing on a stranger's porch.

Laura had said nothing during her meltdown. She'd simply sat silently next to her.

Exactly like her mom used to.

She faced Laura. Up close she could spot a few differences between the twins. Laura had more freckles on her nose and cheeks, which Tiffany would guess was because of all the yard work she did. Her mom had been a nurse and spent many hours inside, but the upside was it made for great sunblock. Laura's left eyebrow had a split in the middle as if it held a long-forgotten scar, and her nose had the slightest bump on the bridge. They were minor differences that the average person might not notice, but Tiffany did.

"You're so like her," she finally told her aunt.

"Like who?" Laura asked.

Her voice remained calm, but Tiffany had caught the sudden way her gaze had shot up, then away, as if she already knew the answer. There had been a little telltale tremor. A quiet sigh. Laura might have guessed Tiffany's identity, but she doubted her aunt knew why she was paying her a surprise visit.

How could Tiffany do this? How could she tell this woman that her identical twin sister was gone?

There was no easy way to break the news. "I'm Tiffany Jackson, your niece. I'm so sorry to tell you this, but your sister passed away."

She'd thought blurting out the truth would hurt less, like ripping a bandage off. But that wasn't true. Pain was pain whether it was delivered fast or slow. If she had any doubts that Laura thought otherwise, Tiffany only had to glance at her aunt to confirm they were in accord.

Laura closed her eyes and sat as still as a statue. Tears spilled down her cheeks. She pressed her thumb and forefinger against her lids to stem the flow and wipe them away. Apparently, it was okay for Tiffany to let it all out, but this woman was as controlled as her mom, if in different ways.

Without meeting Tiffany's eyes, Laura asked, "How?"

"Ovarian cancer." Tiffany took a deep breath. If she started crying again, she'd never stop. "She was diagnosed six months ago. We tried everything—surgery, radiation, and chemotherapy. She fought it, but in the end, it was too much, too far advanced. She died two weeks ago."

When her aunt remained silent, Tiffany went into more detail, telling her of the hopes and prayers. She shared snippets of good times when they thought the treatments were working, and she shared how the last few weeks her mother had been bedridden, weak in body but never in spirit or of mind.

"That explains so much," Laura said.

"I don't follow," Tiffany said.

"I've had this terrible pain in here," her aunt explained, lightly tapping her heart. "And it's been growing. Then about two weeks ago, I woke in so much agony, I thought I was having a heart attack. It stopped suddenly, and the pain shifted. I can only describe it as a lonely ache that wrapped itself around me like a cocoon. I've been trying to figure it out."

"I've read that twins have a special bond," Tiffany said. "Some even know when the other is hurt or sick. Maybe it was your twin bond telling you what happened."

"Or breaking. The final thread snapping."

Neither spoke for a few moments, the only sound filling the air that of a lone bird in a nearby tree.

Tiffany had a million questions about the rift between the sisters. What had happened? What could have possibly come between two women who shared not only a sisterly bond but the deeper connection everyone heard about with twins? How could Laura have walked away from her family? Did she miss them? Think of them?

She also wanted to know about Laura as a person. What did she do for a living? Was she married? Did she have kids? The thought that Tiffany might have cousins filled her with a spark of hope. But she knew right now wasn't the time to bombard her aunt with everything running through her mind. Tiffany had to give Laura time to process the news.

"You were named after our mother," Laura remarked. "Your grandmother would have loved having a namesake. She was a wonderful woman and mother. I can see a bit of her in your eyes. But I digress."

"It's okay," Tiffany said. "I don't mind."

"I'm sorry for your loss," Laura said. "Losing your mother so young is not easy and never fair. I can't imagine Martin took it well."

"We lost my dad five years ago," Tiffany said. "He was hit by a drunk driver. I guess that makes me an orphan now." Her voice shook as those words left her mouth.

She hadn't thought about it before. At least, not in those terms. Nobody called parentless adults orphans, but technically that was what they were. Too many painful memories swirled inside her. She couldn't handle them at the moment, so she pushed them away. Later she'd examine them closer and deal with the emotional trauma. Right now, all she really knew was that she was alone save for this stranger next to her.

"Both your parents are gone?" Laura asked. Her shoulders shook as silent sobs racked her body. "It's too much."

Tiffany sniffled. "I know."

Her aunt rose from her chair and headed toward the house. "Thank you for coming here in person to tell me. It means a lot. But I think I need to go lie down for a bit." She opened the door.

What? She was leaving? But Tiffany hadn't completed her mission. There was still the necklace to deliver. She grabbed her purse. "Wait!"

Laura gave a startled jump and faced her again.

"I've got something for you," Tiffany said, lowering her voice. "It's from my mom. Please give me a minute to find it."

Laura didn't say anything as she returned to her chair.

Tiffany dug around in her purse. Where in the world was the necklace? She took each item out one by one, setting everything on the little wicker table. She turned out the pockets and finally dumped her purse upside down. The necklace was gone.

"It must have fallen out at the inn this morning." She glanced up to meet her aunt's questioning gaze. "My purse fell off the dresser while I was getting ready. Can I come back tomorrow and bring it to you?"

"I imagine you've got a job to get back to and a family of your own," her aunt said. "Why don't you pop it in the mail?"

"But I want to hand-deliver it to you," Tiffany insisted. "My mom's dying wish was for me to tell you she was gone and give you the gift."

"You know, you're a lot like her." Laura grasped the chain of the necklace she wore, though the pendant remained hidden beneath her shirt. "Stubborn as the day is long."

Tiffany smiled. She didn't mind being compared to her mom. It was the highest of compliments in her opinion. "Thank you. I'm still on leave from my job, and I have a few days before I have to go home." She gazed into her aunt's eyes that resembled the ones she knew so well, swallowed her tears, and put her heart on the line. "I don't have a family anymore. Except for you."

She saw her words hit their mark, saw the sting of pain on Laura's face as new tears slid down her cheeks. Her aunt tightened her jaw but remained silent.

Tiffany felt a twinge of guilt, but now that she'd found this missing family member, she wasn't going to walk away without getting to know her better.

And definitely not before she had some answers.

After her aunt agreed to let her return the next day, Tiffany said goodbye and returned to her car. She texted Melinda to let her know that she was leaving her aunt's house.

As Tiffany drove to the inn, she thought about her visit. She understood Laura's need to process the news she'd been given. It had been two weeks since her mom died, and Tiffany was still trying to come to grips with her new reality.

Tiffany was thankful that Laura hadn't shut her out, slammed the door in her face, or threatened to call the police if she didn't leave. It might not have been a warm, loving reunion between two family members, but Tiffany had felt a connection.

The meeting had given her hope.

She had lost both of her parents, but perhaps she wasn't completely alone after all.

Sure, Tiffany had Chris, who was the best boyfriend she could imagine and fully supported her emotional needs during this traumatic ordeal. But while he could empathize with her, he couldn't sympathize. He still had both of his parents as well as his grandparents. He'd never lost anyone he was close to, and honestly, she was very grateful for that.

On the other hand, Laura could sympathize with Tiffany. Even though she and her sister had been estranged for thirty years, they were twins. The loss had clearly cut Laura deeply.

Tomorrow Tiffany wanted to explore the connection she'd felt with her aunt. Hopefully, as they got to know each other, they would learn they had more in common than a blood bond. Maybe they would even like each other and become friends. It would be nice to have an aunt to confide in, to share stories about her and her mom. To go to for advice.

But first Tiffany needed to find the necklace. It had probably ended up under the bed after her purse fell off the dresser and all the contents scattered across the floor.

She parked the car at the inn and wandered around the mansion to take a walk by the lakeshore. It was too pretty to be inside, and she had plenty of time later to search for the missing necklace.

As she came around the corner, she heard Winston's sharp bark.

The dog bounded over to her and planted his little paws on her legs, tail wagging furiously.

It was good to know that someone was happy to see her. "Hey there. What are you up to today?" She bent down to give Winston attention, then heard footsteps. She glanced up to see Charlotte and Grace approaching.

"You're back early," Charlotte remarked. "If you need a pick-me-up, there are chocolate-dipped strawberries and strawberry lemonade in the kitchen."

"That sounds wonderful," Tiffany said. "I'm starving."

"I want to apologize for the torn screen in your room," Grace said. "Charlotte told me about it, and we had it fixed while you were gone."

"It wasn't a big deal," Tiffany said. "But thanks for taking care of it so quickly."

"How did it go with your aunt?" Grace asked.

"It went well," Tiffany said, then amended her statement. "Or at least as well as can be expected since I was the bearer of bad news."

"I can't imagine that was easy for either of you," Grace said, "but I'm sure your aunt loved finding out she has a niece."

"Maybe. It was hard to tell what she was thinking or feeling other than sad, but I understand that." Tiffany gave Winston one last pet and stood up. "I'm going back to see her tomorrow, but I need to locate a missing necklace."

"Missing necklace?" Charlotte echoed with clear concern.

Tiffany explained the situation, assuring both innkeepers that the necklace had most likely fallen under the bed when her purse slid off the dresser.

Tiffany hoped she was right, because if she couldn't find the necklace, not only would she not have an excuse to visit her aunt, but she would have failed her mom again.

8

Melinda

Humming a cheerful tune, Melinda propped the bike against the tree where she'd found it in the front yard at the inn.

As she made her way up the walk, she executed a little dance move she'd learned long ago and then laughed. For not having a job or solid plans for the future, she felt surprisingly light, energetic, and full of joy. Maybe it was the fresh air and sunshine—things she did not get much of working in an office. Or maybe it was her upcoming dinner date, which was another item that had been sorely lacking in her life these past couple of years. Either way, she reveled in her good mood.

Melinda planned to go to her room and take a soak in the tub in the hopes that her long-neglected muscles wouldn't pick the middle of dinner to cramp up. But as she entered the foyer, she heard Grace talking in the other room and decided to pop in and say hello.

At the entrance to the living room she came to a dead stop. Couch cushions were tossed aside, and Winnie ran her hands along the seams. Grace was on her hands and knees as she peeked under a table. Furniture had been shoved to the far side of the room and the carpet rolled up.

Melinda turned to go, not wanting to interrupt or get in the way.

Grace sat up, brushing the hair out of her face, and smiled at Melinda. "How was your bike ride?" She stood and dusted off her knees, casually moving pillows back into place.

"It was great. Thanks again for letting me borrow your bike."

Melinda motioned to the disheveled room. "Are you redecorating or still searching for your missing key?"

"Unfortunately, I'm still looking for the key," Grace answered. "But I thought while we were at it, we'd do a little deep cleaning and rearranging."

"Good plan," Melinda said.

"If you'd like to sit and relax on the back veranda, I could bring you a glass of sweet tea or lemonade," Grace offered. "There's a refreshing breeze coming off the lake."

"Oh no, I'm fine, but thank you. I've got too much energy to sit." Melinda meandered over to a lovely oak side table. She lifted the lid off a crystal candy dish and peered inside. "You did check the freezer, right?"

"The freezer?" Winnie asked. "What in the world would the key be doing in the freezer?"

"Probably the same thing it's doing anywhere else: waiting for me to find it." Grace laughed and unrolled the carpet. "Actually, I did check the freezer. Sadly, I didn't find the key, but I did spy a carton of butter pecan ice cream I'm thinking about indulging in for dinner."

Winnie laughed. "I wish I could join you. It sounds a lot more interesting than baked chicken."

"You're always welcome," Grace said. "You know we always keep sugar-free, low-carb ice cream on hand for you. You're welcome to join me too, Melinda."

"Thank you for the offer, but I have a date tonight."

"Anyone we might know?" Winnie asked.

"Actually, yes. Ryan. I'm sure he simply didn't want to eat alone." Melinda didn't want to assume the date was anything more than that. She'd felt like they'd had a connection, but that didn't mean he saw anything in her other than a nice person to talk to and have dinner with. "He mentioned going to Turner's Lakeside Grill."

"I'm sure you'll enjoy your meal," Grace said. "The food and the service there are top-notch."

"Ryan's been coming here for years, and he's one of our favorite guests," Winnie added. "Sometimes he even goes fishing with my husband, Gus."

"I'm excited about it." Melinda frowned. "But I am a little nervous. It's been a while since my last date. I'm not even sure what to talk about."

"You had dinner last night, didn't you?" Grace sat down on the couch now that it was restored to rights. "What did you talk about then?"

"We discussed what we did for a living," Melinda said, "and he talked about birds and the area. But it was easy because Tiffany was there to fill in the gaps." Actually, with the three of them it had felt like old friends catching up as they bounced from one topic to the next. Melinda hadn't worried about what anyone thought of her, but a date was so much different.

"I think you'll find the conversation flows as smoothly as it did before with only the two of you." Grace stood and walked to a bookshelf. "If all else fails, you can talk about birds. Ryan is quite the ornithologist." She handed Melinda a book on local flora and fauna.

"Thank you. I feel better already." Melinda flipped through the book, then set it down. She wandered around the room, joining Grace and Winnie in their search.

"Can you cut the lock off the shed if we don't find the key?" Winnie asked.

"I could, but it feels wasteful," Grace said. "It has to be around here somewhere. Keys don't get up and walk away on their own. I guess if I don't find it soon, I'll have to cut the lock off. If someone wants to go out on the lake, I'll have no option. The kayaks and the rowboat are stored in there."

"So are some of the supplies for Helen's surprise party," Winnie reminded her.

Melinda's ears perked up at the mention of a party. "Is there anything I can do to help you get ready for the party? I've got nothing but time on my hands."

"That's kind of you to offer, but you're on vacation. I'm sure you have other things to do." Grace pushed a chair into place and moved a vase of flowers. "Speaking of fun things, how is the soul-searching coming along?"

"I've made some progress," Melinda said.

"I'm glad to hear it," Grace responded. "I always find it inspirational to be active outside."

"My best ideas always seem to come when I'm washing dishes," Winnie said with a laugh.

"I've narrowed it down to opening a sewing novelty and supply store or greeting shoppers at a superstore," Melinda said.

"Those are all good choices," Grace said.

"Do you sew?" Winnie asked.

"No, I don't," Melinda said.

"My quilting group, The Busy Bees, meets tomorrow night," Winnie said. "Why don't you join us? It's never too late to learn. Even if you're not interested, it's a friendly bunch, and we love to chat."

"Thanks for asking," Melinda said. "I met Angel today at the Dragonfly, and she extended the same invitation. I love how friendly everyone in Magnolia Harbor is."

"Speaking of sewing, I'm also missing my thimble," Grace said. "Perhaps you could pick up a new one for me when you're at Spool & Thread tomorrow."

"Sure, I can do that." Winnie checked her watch and frowned. "Oh my, I didn't realize how late it was. I need to get home and start dinner. Gus will be waiting."

"Thanks for your help," Grace said, giving her aunt a hug.

"Anytime," Winnie replied. She turned to Melinda. "Enjoy your date tonight." She waved and left the room.

"You were talking about starting a business or landing a job that involves a hobby you like," Grace said. "I think that's a great idea. At least you'd look forward to work every day."

"You're right," Melinda said, pacing the room. "I didn't love accounting, but I'm good at it. It would be nice for my work to also be my passion. I just need to figure out what that is." She stopped pacing and smiled. "But now, I'd better get ready for my date."

"Have a wonderful time with Ryan," Grace said.

"Thanks," Melinda said. "Oh, and I'm serious about helping with the surprise party. I know it's unusual for you to put one of your guests to work, but you'd be doing me a favor. I would love to lend a hand."

"How about we meet after breakfast tomorrow?" Grace suggested. "We can go over my to-do list, and you can fill me in on your date."

"Sounds great." Melinda said goodbye and dashed upstairs to get ready.

Since time had slipped away from her, she had to forgo her long soak in the tub. As it was, she still ran slightly behind schedule.

Melinda selected a retro 1950s pink floral sleeveless dress with a sweetheart neckline and a flared skirt. The heels were modest in pale pink, and she twisted her hair into a loose and low chignon, with strands framing her face. For the first time in weeks, she applied full makeup to play up her gray eyes.

After checking her appearance in the mirror, Melinda hurried downstairs.

When she stepped onto the back veranda, Ryan was already waiting for her. He was handsome in slacks, a sport jacket, and a button-down shirt. The dark-green shirt looked good with his tanned skin and brought out the green in his hazel eyes.

There was a spark of surprise, then delight in Ryan's eyes when he saw her, and he smiled. "You're beautiful."

A warm glow swept over her. "Thank you. You clean up very nicely too."

"Are you ready?" he asked.

Melinda nodded.

Ryan held out his arm and escorted her toward the back steps. "I hope you don't mind a slight change in plans. I tried to make a reservation at Turner's, but they're booked solid tonight."

"No worries," she said. "I'm pretty easy to please. As long as the food is good, so am I."

"I'm glad to hear that."

They kept walking toward the lake. At first, Melinda thought they were going to boat over to The Tidewater for dinner. But as they got closer to the dock, she could see Ryan had other plans.

Her heart stumbled as she took in the romantic scene. A small bistro table and two chairs were set up on the dock. On the table were two place settings, a candle in a tiny lantern, and a vase of colorful flowers. An ice bucket and a picnic basket sat off to the side. Strings of tiny lights hung from the surrounding trees. He'd clearly put a lot of thought and effort into their date.

"Oh, this is perfect," Melinda gushed.

"I'm happy you like it." Ryan ushered her to the table and pulled out a chair for her.

"Thank you," she said as she sat down.

He lifted a bottle of wine from the ice bucket. "Is white okay?"

"That would be lovely," Melinda said. "How did you arrange all of this on such short notice?" No one had ever gone to so much trouble for her on a date before. It was a lovely feeling.

"Grace and Charlotte," Ryan answered, lighting the candle in the center of the table.

"I thought they didn't serve dinner at the inn."

"They don't." A grin lit up his face. "But I've been coming here since they opened the place, and they're both romantics at heart."

Doubt and disappointment unfurled within Melinda. She liked Ryan, but she had no intention of being another vacation fling. "So, you do this often?"

"Do what?"

She gestured toward the table and picnic basket. "Woo other inn guests during your stays."

To his credit, Ryan appeared stunned. Then he laughed. "No, not at all. To be honest, the idea of wooing a woman scares me. It's been a long time."

Melinda tilted her head, searching his eyes for the truth. What she found was a hint of uncertainty, a touch of pain, and a lot of sadness. "Why don't you pour us each a glass of wine and tell me why it's been a long time? I find it hard to imagine why a man who is so funny, kind, and handsome doesn't regularly date."

"Okay, but let's eat while we talk." Ryan filled both glasses, then removed two covered dishes from the picnic basket and placed the dishes in front of each of them. "Since you were torn between the shrimp Caesar salad and the chicken Milano last night, I picked up the salad for dinner so you get to try both."

Melinda grinned. "That's exactly what I was craving."

"To answer your question, I have dated here and there," he said, pulling out a small basket of rolls with a dish of butter. "Mostly, it's because a friend or family member knows the 'perfect person' for me."

"Blind dates. Fun." She raised her glass. "To the well-meaning."

Ryan clinked his glass with hers. "I tried online dating, but I'm too old-fashioned for that method. Swipe left, then right. I could never remember which direction was yes or no. Besides, I could have been half of those women's father. It was kind of scary."

"Have you tried speed dating?" Melinda asked.

"Is that still a thing?" He offered her a roll before taking one for himself.

"Oh yes, and it can be quite complex too," she replied. "I went to one event where we had to match up keys and locks. At another, I was about twenty years younger than all the men. The third and last one I attended took place in a restaurant. The place was packed, and we had six minutes to talk."

"I'm guessing six minutes feels like a lifetime in the wrong situation."

"You're absolutely right. One guy's first question to me was, 'Why are you still single?' Now, I kind of asked you the same thing, but it wasn't my first question."

"What did you tell him?"

"I asked why he was still single," Melinda said with a chuckle. "He got up and walked away without answering. And it was so loud in there. You couldn't hear anyone."

"Was there a band playing?" he asked.

"No, it was karaoke night. Do you know how awkward it is to try to get to know someone when another person is singing love songs over the conversation?"

"This is starting to sound like a comedy," Ryan said.

"Sitcom in the making," she said. "We were all shouting to be heard, leaning into each other's personal space, and some woman was warbling, 'I Will Always Love You.' One date was rating the singer. Another didn't say a word past hello. The last one talked nonstop about the problems with the sanitation transportation system."

"Wow, what an evening."

"But that's not the best part."

"Really?" he asked. "What else happened?"

"The police showed up." Melinda laughed and took a sip of her wine. "So there we were all clustered in a corner of the restaurant, playing musical chairs. The event organizer had just signaled to change dates when the police walked in. No one thought anything of it at first until they approached the organizer."

"Is it illegal to hold an event like that in a public restaurant?" Ryan asked.

"No, but it turned out she'd been running a scam," she said. "She'd been hosting these speed-dating events and peppering the participants with her team. They'd set up real dates, and while the couple was out, the woman's house would get robbed."

"Did anyone get hurt during the robberies?"

"Thankfully, no. But I don't think I'll ever forget that night. The whole time as she's being arrested, she's spouting off how she's doing 'Cupid's work' bringing fated couples together, and the person onstage is singing the theme from the old *Cops* TV show."

He shook his head. "That's crazy."

"Needless to say, I've been hesitant to try speed dating again." Melinda ate a bite of her salad before adding, "I think I prefer the old-fashioned way of letting fate lead you to where you're supposed to be and to the person you're supposed to be with."

Ryan smiled. "Me too. That's how I met my wife."

Slowly, she lowered her fork to the table and swallowed hard. "You're married?" She knew he had been too good to be true.

"I was," he said. "But now I'm widowed."

Melinda covered her face with her hands to hide the blush that had to be filling her burning cheeks. When would she let go of the past and learn to trust again? It had been years, but she still clung to old hurts. She'd even gone to therapy and thought she'd gotten better. And she had, until a few dates had given her plenty of reason to doubt all the pretty words men said when they tried to impress. But her gut kept telling her that Ryan was different.

"I'm sorry for your loss," Melinda said gently. She couldn't even imagine the pain he'd gone through or the strength he had to keep going. "Would you like to tell me about her? What was her name?"

Tears glazed his eyes as a small, sad smile formed. "Beth. We met in ninth grade and hated each other on sight. Then the following year we got paired up in science class. We were together from then on."

"Chemistry class?" Melinda joked, hoping to lighten the mood.

"Actually, yes." His smile grew. "We had our ups and downs, but somehow she stuck with me. We got married right out of college. We made all these grand plans for our future."

She nodded.

"We were so young and full of ourselves," Ryan continued. "But we were dealt the first blow almost immediately. Beth got pregnant. There were complications, and she lost the baby. After that, she wasn't able to have children, so she became a preschool teacher. She said if she couldn't have her own kids to love, it was the next best thing."

"She sounds like a wonderful person," Melinda said. She couldn't help but wonder if Ryan still wanted children. He had to be around her age. If so, she wasn't his ideal candidate at forty-five. It was well past her time.

"She was," he said, a faraway look in his eyes. "Beth was full of contradictions. She loved to travel, but she had the worst sense of direction ever. She hated to fly, but she always dreamed of going to London. And she loved to sing, but she sounded like a cat with its tail caught in the door."

"I'm guessing that didn't stop her from belting out her favorite tunes?" Melinda asked with a grin.

"No, not at all. We had a good life together. A lot of happy times. But then she got the flu." Ryan huffed. "Something that happens all the time. Thousands get it every year, and people die from it, but they're always really young or old. It's easy to believe that it can't happen to someone like Beth."

"I'm so sorry," she said. "It's never fair when people we love are taken too soon, especially someone like Beth who gave back to the world."

"Thank you for saying that," Ryan told her.

They fell into a companionable silence as they finished their salads.

Just as Melinda thought the date would end, Ryan surprised her with dessert and turned the conversation toward more upbeat subjects. They discussed his job as a custom cabinetmaker and woodworker and hers as an accountant. They talked about their hobbies—his love of birds and her passion for reading.

Melinda admitted that she'd been engaged once before, but she'd found out right before the wedding that he wasn't who he pretended to be. She didn't go into details. Somehow they didn't seem important so many years later.

After indulging in slices of French silk pie, Ryan guided Melinda over to a nearby rowboat and helped her get settled. He rowed them out on the lake, not too far from shore, and pointed out various birds.

"I can't believe we live so close to each other, but we had to come all the way to South Carolina to meet," he remarked.

"It is interesting that all three of us staying at the inn are from Georgia," she said. "It's like fate is working some kind of plan."

"I think you're right," Ryan said. "You mentioned earlier that you're in between jobs. Well, I'm in need of a bookkeeper. Mine quit to become a full-time mother. It's clear we get along, so do you think you'd be interested in the job?"

"That's very kind of you," Melinda said. She was grateful for the offer, but she wasn't sure it was a good idea. "Do you mind if I think about it for a couple of days?"

"Of course," Ryan said. "After all, mixing business with pleasure can be tricky at times, but I think we'd be okay."

His comment sent a small thrill through Melinda. She couldn't deny that the more she got to know Ryan, the more she liked him. She was glad to hear he felt the same way, but she wasn't ready to rush into anything.

They discussed movies, sports, and politics, and they discovered that they meshed on many levels.

As they talked, time slipped away, the night sky changing from a dusky pink to inky blue illuminated by the tiny lights strung in the surrounding trees.

Melinda sighed with contentment. She wished this magical evening would never end.

Tiffany

After giving her room one last glance the next morning in the hopes she'd spot the missing necklace, Tiffany let out a frustrated sigh and closed the door. She knew she'd placed it in a side pocket inside her purse before she left home. It had to be in her room, her car, or somewhere in between. She hadn't made any stops on her drive to the inn. It wasn't as if the necklace could have flown away, so it had to be somewhere nearby.

When she went downstairs, Winston raced to greet her with a wagging tail, then sat at her feet, offering his paw.

"Winston, you are the cutest dog ever." Tiffany squatted down to scratch him behind the ears.

After giving Winston her full attention for a few minutes, Tiffany went to the dining room, where Charlotte had set up the breakfast buffet. Something smelled amazing. She followed her nose and lifted the lid off a warming tray. Crepes. One of her all-time favorite foods.

"Those are delicious," Ryan remarked as he entered the room. "I highly recommend them."

"They smell great." She slid two crepes onto her plate, then filled a small bowl with fresh fruit and sprinkled granola over the top with a dollop of yogurt.

"Melinda and I are having breakfast on the back veranda," Ryan said, refilling his coffee. "You should join us. It's a beautiful morning."

"I'd love to." Tiffany followed Ryan outside. It was nice to enjoy the fresh air before returning to work. She sat down at the table with Ryan and Melinda and took a moment to silently say grace.

"Are you okay?" Melinda asked her. "I hate to say it, but you look a little tired."

"I am," Tiffany said. "I didn't sleep very well last night."

Grace and Charlotte stepped outside in time to hear her comment.

"Oh no," Grace said. "Was the bed not comfortable?"

"The bed isn't the problem. I couldn't shut my brain down." Tiffany had been mentally retracing her steps, trying to figure out where the necklace could be.

"I have a great tea blend that will help you sleep," Charlotte said. "I'll leave it on the counter in the kitchen. If I'm not around when you're ready, let Grace know, and she can make it for you."

"Thank you. I might take you up on that," Tiffany said. "It would also help if I could find my mom's necklace. I know it was in my purse when I left home, but when I got to my aunt's house, it wasn't there." It gave her the perfect excuse for a second visit, but she had to locate it soon so she could fulfill her mom's dying wish.

"Did you search your room?" Grace asked.

Tiffany nodded. "I thought the necklace landed under the bed or something when my purse fell to the floor yesterday. But no luck."

"What kind of box is it in?" Ryan asked.

"It's not in a box," Tiffany said. "I wish I'd thought of that. It would be easier to find."

"It might have fallen out in your car," Melinda suggested.

"I'm going to double-check my car and the path from my car to the house," Tiffany said. "If you all could keep an eye out too, I would appreciate it. It's a gold arrow with an amethyst."

The group promised to watch for the necklace.

Charlotte and Grace made sure their guests had everything

they needed, then went back inside with Winston trotting along after them.

Tiffany, Melinda, and Ryan chatted about nothing in particular for a few minutes as Tiffany bit into the most scrumptious crepes—ham, cheese, and spinach—she'd ever had.

As Ryan got up to leave, he called a greeting to a good-looking man with salt-and-pepper hair and an adorable chocolate Lab. The men shook hands.

"Ladies, let me introduce you to Spencer Lewis," Ryan said, then dropped down to pet the dog. "And this is Bailey."

Spencer greeted Tiffany and Melinda and asked if they were enjoying their stay, then gave them a few suggestions on local attractions to visit.

"Gus and I are going fishing tomorrow morning," Ryan told Spencer. "Do you feel like joining us?"

"Sure," Spencer said. "Do you want to take my boat? It'll hold three people more comfortably than Grace's rowboat."

The men finalized their plans to meet early the next morning, and Spencer promised to update Gus on the time and location. Then Spencer went into the inn with Bailey on his heels, and Ryan left to meet with his client.

"Want some help searching for your lost necklace?" Melinda offered.

"Yes, if you don't have anything better to do," Tiffany said. "Maybe with two of us on the hunt, we'll discover it."

They walked through the inn and out the front door to retrace Tiffany's steps.

"How did your meeting with your aunt go?" Melinda asked as she scanned the ground.

"You mean my mother's *twin* sister?" Tiffany asked.

Melinda stopped. "I'm guessing by the way you said twin, your mom didn't tell you."

"Nope, but she was in pretty bad shape at the end." Tiffany wiped an errant tear from her cheek and opened her eyes wide to fight off the flood of tears that threatened to fall. "It was worse than staring at a ghost. They even sound alike."

"Oh no," Melinda said. "I'm so sorry you had to go through that, especially alone."

"I appreciate it," Tiffany said. "Once I recovered from the shock, I was able to spot a few differences between my mom and my aunt. They don't amount to much, but it was enough that I got into a better mindset. It was also hard on my aunt when I told her the news."

"That's to be expected. Did the two of you get a chance to talk?" Melinda resumed her search of the ground as they made their way from the front steps to Tiffany's car.

"Not really. She needed some time to process everything," Tiffany answered. "I have so many questions. She's the only family I have left, and I'd really like to get to know her."

"Then do it," Melinda urged. "Spend the rest of your trip with your aunt."

"I will," Tiffany said. "I booked the room until the weekend, but initially I thought I'd probably leave right after I met her. I mean, if she hasn't come around in thirty years, she doesn't want anything to do with me, right?"

"Maybe not," Melinda said. "I'm sure whatever kept her from home all these years has nothing to do with you. Maybe she's been waiting for an excuse. Or some kind of olive branch that never came until now."

Tiffany had had those exact same thoughts during the night while she'd tossed and turned and counted sheep. She hoped both she and Melinda were correct.

They covered the distance to her car with no sign of the necklace.

Unlocking the doors, Tiffany took the driver's side, and Melinda started searching the passenger side.

"I hope I'm not wasting my time here, because I really should be at work," Tiffany remarked. "They've held my position for the past two months while I took care of Mom, but if I don't return by the end of this month, there's no guarantee I'll still have a job."

"It's a shame that not all companies offer bereavement leave," Melinda said. "But after working in accounting all these years, I also understand that some operate on a very tight budget."

Tiffany was outside the car on her knees, and she leaned forward, resting her arms on the cushion of the driver's seat. "Can I make a confession?"

"Sure." Melinda sat on the passenger seat and looked at her.

"I don't care if they give my job away. These past couple of months were the worst of my life, but they were also kind of nice." Tiffany sat back to rest on her heels, letting the morning sun warm her face. "This feels so good, being outside and getting fresh air. And I love this view."

"It is gorgeous here," Melinda agreed.

"I like my work, and I'm good at it," Tiffany said. "But I don't enjoy sitting under fluorescent lights staring at a computer screen all day. I also don't care for the tiny cubicles that block me from seeing other people and limit all my interactions to e-mails or instant messaging. Working in an office gets old fast."

Melinda nodded and moved her search to the back seat. "Accounting is much the same. You study spreadsheets and forms for eight to ten hours a day. No one wants to talk to you because they're afraid to mess up your concentration, which means messed-up numbers. It gets lonely. So, yes, I get it."

With no luck finding the necklace on the ground or in the car, both women walked slowly back to the inn. Melinda seemed a little lost in her own thoughts, and Tiffany had an idea as to why.

"How did your date with Ryan go last night?" Tiffany asked. "Did you like Turner's Lakeside Grill?"

"We didn't go to the restaurant," Melinda replied.

"What? Why not?"

"Ryan couldn't get a reservation, so he planned a candlelight picnic on the dock."

"How romantic," Tiffany said. It made her wish Chris was with her on this trip. His calls and texts helped, but she missed him so much. She'd have to get used to being apart after he deployed in a month.

"It was incredibly sweet and thoughtful," Melinda said, sounding surprised and delighted. "The evening was a little romantic, but most of all it was fun and easy."

"I'm glad you took my advice to forget about your problems for a while and have a good time," Tiffany said. "A fall romance might help to pull you out of your slump."

Melinda laughed and flushed a lovely shade of pink. "It's nothing like that. We had dinner together and talked."

"Is that all?"

"Well, we went on a boat ride," Melinda admitted. "It was a nice way to end the date."

"You called it a date. I knew there was something between you two." Tiffany bumped Melinda's shoulder and laughed. "I'm thrilled for you. He seems really nice."

"He is," Melinda said, "but don't get your hopes up. We didn't make any other plans, so it might have been our first and last date."

"We'll see," Tiffany teased. "For now, what do you have planned for the day?"

"I'm hoping to persuade Grace to let me help with a surprise party she's planning, and then I might take the bike back into town. I'd like to check out The Book Cottage. How about you?"

"I'm going to my aunt's, even though I can't give her the necklace." Butterflies filled her stomach as she thought about all the questions she wanted to ask Laura. "Do you think I should ask her about the rift between her and my mom?"

"I wouldn't right away," Melinda advised. "Try to let the conversation happen organically. I'd only push the subject if she clearly avoids it and it's still bothering you. Keep in mind that it could be something very personal and embarrassing."

"Thanks. That's a good idea." Feeling a little more settled, Tiffany dug her keys out of her purse. "After all, we don't want her thrusting the sins of the mother onto the daughter. At least not until I know if I deserve them or not."

10

Melinda

Grace was arranging flowers in the living room when Melinda walked in with her laptop.

"How was your date with Ryan?" Grace asked. She motioned to the sofa. "Did you enjoy the picnic on the dock?"

"It was the nicest evening I've had in ages." Melinda sat down. "Thank you for your part in it."

"I'm so glad you had a good time," Grace said, smiling.

"Now please put me to work on the surprise party."

"Are you sure you want to help?" Grace asked. "It's not our policy to ask our guests to work. Besides, you're on vacation, and you're supposed to be relaxing."

"I've been on vacation for months," Melinda said. "I'm going stir-crazy."

"All right," Grace said, retrieving a piece of paper from an end table and handing it to Melinda. She took a seat in a nearby chair. "You can take a peek at my to-do list."

Melinda scanned the list. "It looks good."

"Thanks." Grace sighed. "Charlotte and I have been busy lately, and it's hard to keep track of who is doing what for the party."

"I can make a spreadsheet to keep track of your tasks," Melinda offered. "It's not a big deal. I could do it in my sleep."

"I guess it wouldn't hurt for you to make a simple spreadsheet," Grace said. "It would help me out, and more importantly, it would make you happy."

Melinda grinned. "Very happy."

Grace chuckled and passed over the rest of her notes. She gave Melinda permission to add anything that she'd forgotten. "Charlotte can double-check it later, and we'll edit as needed. I'd like to keep it as a template for future parties."

"I'll get right on it," Melinda said, opening her laptop. "Thanks for giving me something to do this morning."

"Thanks for offering to help." Grace went back to arranging flowers. "I'm surprised you're free this morning. I thought you and Ryan might go out exploring."

"He had a meeting with his client." Melinda settled into her task as she recalled the steps she'd gone through to plan her parents' fiftieth anniversary party. It had been a huge success as well as a huge undertaking.

Grace fetched two cups of coffee, then focused on her own work.

Melinda created the spreadsheet, adding the ability for the automatic cost calculation to one column and per price cost to another before saving the document. When she was finished, she glanced up to see that Grace was done with the flowers and had set out a plate of snickerdoodles.

As Melinda explained what she'd done, the two of them munched on the cookies.

"This is fabulous," Grace said. "So much more detailed than I expected. You're really good. Maybe instead of finding a new job, you should go into business for yourself."

"I've thought about it. The idea definitely has merit, and I've even got a potential first customer—Ryan." Melinda shrugged. "But I'm not sure if I want to keep doing the same old thing, even if I have a knack for it. I kind of fell into accounting by accident. The job was supposed to be temporary, until the company filled a position and I figured out what I wanted to do."

The problem was, it was now more than twenty-five years later, and she still hadn't figured out that dream yet. It made her wonder if she ever would or if she was one of those people who didn't have a passion for anything. Was she a jack-of-all-trades, master of none? No, she was a master of numbers, but she didn't like it anymore.

Melinda sighed. It was like being seventeen all over again and contemplating what to do with her life.

"I understand what you're going through," Grace said. "I was doing well in marketing, but there came a day when it wasn't as satisfying as it should have been anymore. You'll discover what to do next. Just let it come naturally."

"I'll try," Melinda promised. "Thanks for letting me help."

Now that Melinda had exercised her mind, it was time to exercise the rest of her. With Grace's permission, she headed outside to retrieve the bicycle again to ride into town.

First, she stopped to play with Winston and his tennis ball. After a good five minutes of fetching the ball, the dog trotted up the steps and into the house. Melinda took that as her cue that she was excused.

It was a gorgeous day with blue skies, dotted with fluffy white clouds, and the sun was shining. The forecast called for temperatures to remain in the low eighties, making it the perfect day for outside activities, and she planned to enjoy every minute. As she pedaled down the long driveway, a car turned in. She pulled over, then grinned when she recognized the driver.

Ryan stopped the car and rolled down the window. "Just the person I wanted to see."

Melinda tried to ignore the little somersault her heart did at his words. "How did your meeting go?"

"Great. If you don't have anything else planned, I was hoping we could spend the rest of the day together. Maybe go explore the area."

"Sounds wonderful. Let me return the bike."

After parking the bicycle where she found it, Melinda ran inside the mansion to let Grace know of her change in plans. She didn't want the innkeeper to worry when she spotted the bike outside and didn't see her guest anywhere around.

As Ryan and Melinda drove, he caught her up on his meeting and the project. He had so much passion in his voice as he talked that Melinda was slightly envious. She wished she felt that excited about something.

Melinda settled back in her seat, letting the warm air from the open windows caress her skin as she relaxed. Ryan seemed to know the area, and it was nice not to have to worry about which way to go for once. Actually, she hadn't even bothered to ask if he had a destination in mind. She was tired of thinking of the future, and for the moment, she reveled in the present.

Soon Ryan headed off the main road and passed a sign for the barbecue festival.

"Grace mentioned this festival when I checked in," she said.

"I hope you don't mind," Ryan said. "I thought it would be fun. They have some great food, arts and crafts vendors, and later on there's a band."

"Sounds good." Melinda glanced down at her white blouse, pale-blue capris, and white tennis shoes. If history was any kind of predictor, by the end of the day, she'd have at least one stain on her shirt, another on her pants, and her favorite sneakers would be filthy. She'd simply have to avoid eating if she had any hope of saving her outfit.

Ryan parked the car and got out. He opened the door for her and held out his arm, a shy smile inviting her to take a chance.

She stepped out, took his arm, and met his gaze. "Shall we go see what this barbecue festival is all about? I hope we weren't supposed to come in pig costumes."

He chuckled as he led the way from the parking lot toward the noise on Main Street. "I believe costumes are optional."

"Oh, that's a relief," Melinda teased. "I left my snout and tail at home since Halloween isn't until next month."

Ryan eyed her as if he were trying to figure out if she was serious or not. "Do you normally dress up for Halloween?"

"Every year," she said. "The kids in my neighborhood love coming to my house. They get full-size candy bars and never know who is going to answer the door. It could be a witch or a monster or a cartoon character. The parents get hot cider and doughnuts because goodness knows they need the carbs to keep up with their little goblins that night."

"What's this year's theme? Spooky or funny?"

Melinda sidestepped a mom pushing a stroller containing a cranky toddler, with an energetic Jack Russell terrier in tow. "I'm not sure. Usually, I start working on my costume long before now, but I haven't been inspired. Maybe I'll skip the costume this time."

"Or maybe you'll find your inspiration here at the festival," Ryan suggested, motioning to the many vendors set up before them. "Does your house get the full makeover too?"

"Not really." She walked toward the row of vendors. "I live in an old Victorian in town, so it would be perfect. The problem is finding the time to make the decorations, then put them up and take them down afterward."

They stopped at a jewelry tent and browsed the wares. There was everything from bracelets made from volcanic rocks to earrings made of sea glass. A set containing earrings, a necklace, and a bracelet all made from pastel-colored glass caught her attention, and she moved around the table to get a better look. It would make a fabulous Christmas present for her mom.

"What do you do for Christmas decor?" Ryan asked as if he'd read her mind.

"I go all out," she said. "Of course, this year, lack of time isn't really a problem. What about you? Do you decorate your house for Halloween?"

"I don't get any trick-or-treaters at my place," he said. "I'm not in a neighborhood, and my house sits too far back from the main road. But I always set up a display for the holidays. Lots of lights."

"You don't have a goal of having your house seen from space, do you?" Melinda asked. She examined the set and decided to buy it.

"No." Ryan laughed. "Nothing quite that crazy, just something for people to enjoy as they drive by. Maybe a life-size sleigh and reindeer cutouts lit up by several trees. Oh, and I added a train last year. The kids seem to get a kick out of it."

"Is that all?" Melinda asked with a smile.

He scratched his chin slowly, seeming to search his memory. "In the yard, yes. Now on top of the house there's a cutout of the Grinch with his sack of presents and his dog, Max."

"All of this is for the *children's* enjoyment who drive by, right?" she teased.

"Sure, and my nieces and nephews when they come over," Ryan said. "I host a family holiday party at my place, and they love it."

Melinda laughed. "I'm thinking Uncle Ryan loves it as much as they do."

"You're right," he admitted.

"There's nothing wrong with that," she said. "If I had your woodworking skills, I'd do the same with my yard."

Once they finished perusing the jewelry, Melinda handed the set and her credit card to the vendor.

"Nice choice," the woman said as she wrapped the pieces and slid them into a small bag.

"They're beautiful," Melinda told her. "My mom will love them."

"I'm glad to hear that." The vendor smiled as she passed Melinda her credit card and the small bag.

Melinda thanked the woman, then slipped her arm through Ryan's. "Now, let's go see what else this place has to offer."

They exited the tent and strolled up and down the vendor aisles, stopping to check out various arts and crafts on display. Both bought a few early Christmas and birthday gifts. Melinda skillfully evaded the food tents, hoping that by the time they'd seen everything, she could talk Ryan into going somewhere else with real plates and silverware and sturdy tables. So she could save her outfit and avoid making herself look like a fool.

Melinda spied the most amazing blown glass balls. Some were clustered in bowls, others on sticks, and a few hung from wrought iron trees. The ones that caught her attention were strung up like a wind chime. She gently touched them, smiling at the soothing sounds they made.

"Won't they break?" she asked the vendor.

"I wouldn't leave them out during a storm," she replied, "but otherwise they should be fine."

"Wouldn't they be gorgeous hanging on a front porch?" Melinda asked Ryan. When he didn't respond, she turned to see him chatting with Grace and Spencer, the man she'd met that morning.

"I see you've found my favorite vendor," Grace said.

"All these lovely colored spheres called out to me," Melinda said. "I was admiring this wind chime."

"It's beautiful. You should get it. It would be a wonderful reminder of your trip." Grace put her hand on Spencer's arm. "I'd like you to meet Melinda Rainey. She's staying at the inn this week."

"We met briefly this morning," Spencer told Grace. He turned to Melinda. "Hello again. Are you enjoying the festival?"

Melinda held up her treasure trove of bags and grinned. "Yes. I've got half of my Christmas shopping and one birthday already done. How about you two? It's nice to see you away from the inn, Grace."

"I'm surprised you were able to get her away," Ryan teased.

"I had a little help from Winnie," Spencer said. "She shooed both Grace and Charlotte out the door and told them not to come back until it was time for hospitality hour."

"I think she wanted some quiet time," Grace said. "Gus is building a model train set in their living room."

The others laughed.

Grace picked out several items for her garden, and the vendor wrapped them up.

Spencer took the bag and her free hand in his, then nodded at Melinda and Ryan. "We'd ask you to join us for lunch, but we already ate. I highly recommend PJ's pulled pork. It's the best barbecue around."

Both Melinda and Ryan thanked him for the recommendation and waved as they headed in the opposite direction.

"Are you hungry?" Ryan asked.

Melinda glanced down at her pristine white blouse with a grimace. "I can wait," she said. But then her stomach growled, giving her away.

He chuckled. "Are you sure about that?"

"Maybe we should try PJ's or at least see what other options there are," Melinda said. She hoped one of the restaurants had salad or a corn dog. If she didn't put any mustard or ketchup on it, there was less chance of making a mess.

They followed their noses and the smell of roasting pork, baked beans, barbecue sauce, melted butter, and all things fried. Melinda was disappointed not to see a single offering of salad. Finally, she caved and ordered the pulled pork plate along with Ryan. The smell alone made her mouth water and her stomach grumble, and she knew she wouldn't be satisfied with anything less.

Ryan, always the gentleman, carried both plates to a nearby picnic table.

However, as Melinda took her plate, a toddler crashed into her legs, throwing her off-balance. To avoid landing on the child, Melinda reached for the table, dropping her plate right onto Ryan's lap.

And she'd been worried about ruining her clothes.

Aghast and embarrassed, Melinda covered her mouth and tried not to cry as she repeatedly apologized to Ryan.

"No worries," he assured her. "There's no use crying over spilled beans. Sit tight, and I'll be right back." He walked away.

Melinda sat down and put her head in her hands, wondering how she could have messed up their date so horribly. She expected Ryan to come back any minute and say he was ready to return to the inn.

Instead, when he rejoined her at the table, he held another plate of food. His jeans had a stain, but he didn't seem to care.

"Don't you want to leave?" Melinda asked. She knew her face was red, and she wanted to crawl under a rock and hide.

"No," Ryan said. "Why?"

"Look at your pants."

He glanced down and laughed. "Are you worried that people might accuse me of wasting good barbecue? Actually, that is pretty offensive around here."

"I'm serious."

"So am I."

His mock grin was so ridiculous she had to laugh. "You're not mad at me?"

"Of course not. It was an accident, and the jeans will wash. Are you enjoying the festival?"

Melinda nodded. "I love going to festivals, with the exception of the food. Not that I don't love the food, because I do. It's that they tend to serve them on flimsy plates, and I usually end up dropping something on my shirt. Thanks for taking one for me this time."

"You're welcome." Ryan pushed her new plate toward her and smiled. "My wife and I didn't frequent festivals. We did in the beginning, and then after a while, she'd always squash the idea. Said it was the same old thing."

"What did she want to do instead?" she asked.

"She loved all kinds of art galleries. Mostly paintings and sculptures."

"There aren't a lot of those in Magnolia Harbor," Melinda noted.

"No, but she loved to sit on Grace's back veranda reading with the sun shining down over the lake," he responded. "She said it brought her peace."

"She didn't go bird-watching with you?" she asked, surprised.

He shook his head.

They talked some more with Ryan sharing bits of his life with Beth. Even though it didn't sound like they'd had much in common, it seemed like it had been a happy marriage. When Ryan's smile drooped at the corners, Melinda understood that he might be ready to move on, but he still missed his wife and what they had. Melinda didn't blame him.

"I think Beth would have liked you," he said.

Melinda didn't know what to say. Before she could come up with a response, they heard someone call their names.

Charlotte walked over with a tall, dark-haired man with a five-o'clock shadow. "Ryan, you know Dean."

The two men exchanged pleasantries.

"Dean owns The Tidewater and is the head chef there," Charlotte told Melinda. She nudged Dean with her elbow. "He's not as good in the kitchen as I am, but he's not bad."

Melinda grinned. "Actually, I have sampled his cooking, and I have to say it's pretty tasty. We had dinner there my first night in town. Delicious chicken Milano, by the way."

"Thank you." Dean flashed her a thousand-watt smile. "Always nice to meet a fan." He gave Charlotte a smug look.

Charlotte rolled her eyes. "I see you guys found PJ's pulled pork. It's wonderful, but don't get too full. I prepared some great appetizers for you to try tonight during hospitality hour."

"You always make great appetizers," Ryan said.

"I agree," Melinda chimed in.

"Oh, I'm going fishing tomorrow morning with Spencer and your uncle," Ryan said to Charlotte. "Do you think you could put together a little something for us to take along? Maybe some muffins and fruit and a thermos of hot coffee. I worry about Gus going so long without eating in the morning."

"Sure, it's all about Gus." Charlotte laughed. "But yes, I'll prepare a basket for you. What time are you heading out?"

"We're supposed to meet at Spencer's dock at six," Ryan said.

"Okay, I'll have it ready by five thirty."

"Sounds good," Ryan said. "Thank you."

"I expect a five-star review this year." Charlotte winked, then turned to Melinda. "Thank you so much for that party spreadsheet you created for Grace today. It's going to be a lifesaver going forward."

"It was my pleasure," Melinda said. "If there's anything else I can do to help, let me know."

"Just keep raving about my cooking," Charlotte said. "And give me your opinion on tonight's snack bites because I'm testing them out for the surprise party."

"That I can do," Melinda said.

"I promised Charlotte a visit to her favorite booth, so we better get moving," Dean said, putting his arm around Charlotte's shoulders. "Enjoy the festival."

When they were gone, Ryan gave Melinda an admiring smile. "You're always on the go and making new friends."

Melinda was confused by his comment. Wasn't that why people went on vacation? To explore new places and meet people?

"You're the exact opposite of Beth," he added.

Although Melinda had already realized that Ryan and Beth hadn't had much in common, she was still taken aback. What had brought such an unlikely couple together?

And if he'd been so happily married to his complete opposite, what were the chances he'd go for someone like Melinda when they had so much in common?

11

Tiffany

Tiffany parked in front of her aunt's house. She took a deep breath and exhaled, then got out of the car. As she strode toward the front porch, she straightened her shoulders, lifted her chin, and smiled, determined to make her second meeting go well.

Most of her bravado came from a quick text from Chris. Nothing important, just his daily message saying how much he missed her. His kind words and her chat with Melinda had really helped. She didn't know what it was about her new friend, but despite their age gap, they clicked.

"I'm over here," Laura called from the side yard.

Following the voice and low strains of music that she suddenly noticed, Tiffany found her aunt sitting on the grass in front of her flower bed with a pair of shears in her hand. "Good morning. Can I help?"

A flash of emotion that Tiffany couldn't name caused Laura's whole body to freeze before she resumed her carefree posture.

"You don't have your mother's black thumb, do you?" Laura asked. "I swear plants would wither as soon as that girl walked into a room."

Tiffany laughed as she popped a deadhead off the bush before her. "Growing up, I remember begging to get a Christmas tree the day after Thanksgiving, but she wouldn't let us pick one out until the weekend before. It was always dead within two weeks."

"I'm surprised she didn't buy one of those fake ones."

"Oh, she wanted to, but Dad and I wouldn't have it," Tiffany said. "It wasn't until I was around twelve that I figured out why we didn't have any live plants in the house. That was the year I bought her an African violet for Mother's Day."

"How long did it last?"

"Until I went to college. It was dead by Thanksgiving break. She forgot to water it."

"Well, at least she didn't forget to water you while you were growing up," Laura said.

Tiffany dropped a handful of dead blooms into the nearby basket and sat up on her knees. Her jeans would be covered in dirt, but she didn't care. "She was a much better mother than gardener."

"She was always better with people than I was."

Tiffany regarded her aunt's lush yard and the remnants of her garden. It was clear Laura had a talent with plants. "Is that why you moved to the middle of nowhere?"

"This isn't nowhere," Laura protested. "This is peace and quiet. It's music to my ears, a soothing balm to my soul. It's a sanctuary."

Tiffany studied the yard with fresh eyes. She observed the reading nook under the tree, nestled in the shade with the fountain bubbling nearby to help keep the Southern heat at bay. She heard the birds overhead sing a sweet song. She smelled the freshly cut grass. And she felt the tension start to drain away. Maybe she had a touch of her aunt in her after all. She could see this place as a personal park.

"I didn't mean to insult you," Tiffany said. "You have a beautiful yard and home."

"It's not what your mama would have lived in." Laura chuckled. "Trust me. I know. We may look alike, but we've been different from the moment we came into this world. She screamed and flailed, and I was quiet and ready to snuggle in our mother's arms."

"She did have a strong set of lungs," Tiffany said softly as one memory after another assaulted her.

"And a temper to go with it," Laura added. "But she was quick to burn and quick to flame out."

It was wonderful to have someone to talk to about her mom again, someone who had known her, who understood her. Someone who had loved her. Tiffany had been afraid to say too much, afraid that Laura would shut down at any moment and end their visit before Tiffany was ready. She was determined to know her last relative and learn more about her family, so she let Laura lead the conversation.

Laura nodded for her to move down to the next patch that needed weeding and deadheading. As they worked, they talked, interspersing nonessential topics like how she wasn't deadheading right with Laura's childhood memories of her sister.

"How's the inn you're staying at?" Laura asked after a long silence.

"Stunning." Tiffany smiled. "It's an old mansion converted into a bed-and-breakfast. The owners are extremely nice, and one of them is an amazing chef." She laughed. "I'm pretty sure I've already gained five pounds from sampling her food."

"You must be staying with Grace Porter and Charlotte Wylde."

Tiffany stopped working and faced her aunt. "You know them?"

"I know of them," Laura answered. "Most people around here do. The inn and Charlotte's cooking are well-known. Plus, I used to work at the courthouse. So, when someone files a plan to renovate an old mansion like theirs and turn it into an inn, people talk."

"What did you do at the courthouse?" Tiffany asked. This was the first real tidbit Laura had shared about her life, and Tiffany wanted to hear more. She wanted to hear everything.

"I was a county clerk. Filed forms, sent out notices, took payments." Laura shrugged. "Nothing exciting. I didn't do anything as important as saving lives like your mama and daddy."

"Every job is important, no matter how small. That's what Mom used to say."

"It's what our daddy used to tell us." Laura dusted off her hands and stood, brushing the dirt, leaves, and twigs off her jeans. "Did you find what your mother wanted you to give me? What was it?"

Tiffany sighed. "It's a necklace, and I haven't found it yet."

"Don't fret over it," Laura said, her voice trembling with the tears that shimmered in her eyes. "You'll find it when you least expect it, or it's gone for good. If you do discover it, you can mail it to me." She yanked an errant weed out of the flower bed. "Or you can keep it for yourself. Something of your mama's to remember her by."

Tiffany focused quietly on her own task. Her mom's note hadn't explained why the necklace was so important. Tiffany still wondered why her mother's last wish was for Tiffany to take the necklace to her sister. But Tiffany was afraid to ask Laura. Clearly, based on her aunt's tears, it meant even more than Tiffany had realized.

One way or another, she'd find the necklace and make sure it got to her aunt.

For a while they worked in silence. Small talk slowly crept back into the space between them. Tiffany told Laura about Winston. She shared how the sweet dog filled her heart with love and how she was worried about Chris's upcoming deployment.

"Maybe you should get a Winston of your own," Laura suggested.

"Actually, Mom had a dog named Daisy. She's staying with a neighbor right now, but she'll come live with me when I get back. At least that way I'll have someone waiting at home to greet me each night and to share dinner with."

"Living alone can be a lonely existence even for an introvert," Laura said.

"You never fell in love?" Tiffany asked. "Never got married or had kids?"

"Once a long time ago, I fell in love."

"What happened?"

"Now that's a story that's going to need some sweet tea and molasses cookies. Let's head up to the porch and take a break." Laura pushed herself off the ground, groaning a bit as her joints popped.

Tiffany followed her aunt to the porch. She took a seat on the wicker rocker after her aunt declined her help in the kitchen. It was nice to sit outside, letting the afternoon sun warm her face. A soft breeze flitted across the porch. In the corner of the yard, two squirrels chased each other up and down a tree with bright-red leaves. She could see why Laura thought of this place as a sanctuary. If Tiffany didn't love the convenience of city life, she could totally live out in the country.

"Here you go." Laura set a plate of molasses cookies on the side table and handed her a tall glass that had already started to sweat. "It's peach tea."

"Thank you," Tiffany said. She took a sip of tea. "This is very good."

Laura sat next to her, cradling her own glass of tea. "Are you sure you want to hear my love story? There's no happily ever after in it."

Tiffany set her glass down and picked up a cookie that she broke in half, more to stall than anything else. The way Laura hesitated over her words and the sadness in her voice made Tiffany think twice. Maybe she should let sleeping dogs lie.

After a moment, she asked, "Does your story have something to do with the rift between you and Mom?"

"Oh, sweet child, it's the beginning, middle, and end."

"Then yes, but only if it won't be too painful for you and you think I have a right to know." Tiffany dropped the uneaten cookie on a napkin and grabbed Laura's hands. "If you don't want to tell me, I understand."

"Isn't that why you're here? To learn the truth?"

"No," Tiffany said. "I mean, I'm curious as to what could destroy the bond between twin sisters, but I want to get to know you. You're my aunt, my blood—"

"And part of your mother." Laura patted her hand and smiled. "If you want to know and understand me, then you need to learn what brought me to this place."

"The good, the bad, and the ugly?" Tiffany asked.

"Something like that. Actually, it's quite simple. It's an age-old tale of two sisters in love with the same man."

"My dad?" Tiffany asked, stunned.

Her aunt nodded. "Martin Anthony Jackson was the most handsome and charming man I'd ever met. He was the same for your mom. Of course, we didn't know we'd fallen for the same man until it was too late."

Tiffany couldn't believe her ears. "My dad two-timed you?"

"I don't think he meant to at first," Laura replied. "Most people couldn't tell us girls apart."

Tiffany snorted. "The scar running through your left eyebrow should have been a dead giveaway. You also have more freckles than she did, and there's the bump on the bridge of your nose."

"That's easy for you to notice," Laura said. "You've had a lifetime to memorize your mother's face. Martin and I had dated for only about a week when the two of them met."

"If he loved you, he would have noticed."

"True."

The air cooled as the sun slipped behind a patch of gray clouds. Tiffany shivered. "Did your heart break when he chose my mom?"

Laura sighed. "No, my heart broke when Donna chose Martin over me."

Tears slipped down Tiffany's cheeks, and she looked away. How could her mom have turned her back on her own sister? Granted, she had loved her husband until her last breath, but still, Laura was her twin. "Do you mind telling me what happened?"

"Your mom wanted to be a nurse ever since we were kids," Laura began. "While she killed every plant she touched, she tended to every dog, cat, and creature that would let her near. She got a full scholarship to Georgia State University. It was close enough that she could come home whenever she wanted."

"What were you doing at that time?"

"I spent two years at a community college," Laura replied. "I didn't want to return to school, so I got a job at the police station. I didn't do anything exciting, just typed and answered phones."

"My dad was a cop, so was that how you met him?"

Laura nodded. "Martin was so dashing in his police uniform."

"He was handsome in those dress blues." Tiffany smiled as she remembered her dad dressing up for work functions. When her mom gazed at him, she would always get a dreamy look on her face, her eyes filled with love and pride.

"He got assigned the beat in our neighborhood, and he took the time to get to know the people who lived there," Laura went on. "He used to walk me home. That man could make me laugh at the silliest things."

"He loved to make people laugh," Tiffany agreed. "He said it was the best sound in the world."

"Your dad was a good man."

"But—"

"But nothing," Laura said, cutting her off. "What happened between us doesn't change the fact that he was fundamentally a good person." She took a long sip of her tea and stared at the yard as if watching the past unfold. "Finally, after months of talking and flirting, he asked me out."

"Did you tell my mom about it?" Tiffany asked. "I would think a first date would be pretty newsworthy."

"No, I didn't have a chance to tell her," Laura said. "She didn't come home that week. She had midterms to study for, and she'd been interning at the hospital. She came back for spring break, but we had opposite schedules and didn't see each other. I'd been moved to evenings, and she was gone during the day."

"So, how did my parents meet?" Tiffany asked, confused. "They told me it was serendipity."

Laura laughed. "I guess it was. She was walking home, and he saw her. At first, Martin thought it was me. When she acted like she didn't know him, he played along. Martin and I were on opposite shifts too. He saw her again the next day and the next. As they talked, he realized it wasn't me, but he'd already fallen for her."

"Did he say anything to my mom about you?" Tiffany asked.

"Not that I know of," Laura said. "Maybe he hadn't had a chance or he was waiting to see which one of us he liked better. I didn't give him time. Finally, Donna and I had a free night together, but before I could tell her about my guy, she told me about hers."

"Oh no."

"Oh yes, and she said she was in love."

"After only a week?" Tiffany asked.

Laura snorted. "I said the same thing. I'd had months to get to know him. But she swore she'd found her soul mate."

"What happened next?"

"Well, there was no way I'd let a man come between my sister and me," Laura said. "We were twins, best friends. No one in the world meant more to me than Donna. I canceled my date with Martin the next day, explaining that I couldn't break my sister's heart. He said he understood, and I thought that meant he wouldn't come between us." She bit her lip. "I was so wrong."

"How so?" Tiffany whispered.

"Two months later, Martin and Donna were engaged. I tried to tell her about Martin and me, but we just had a huge fight about it. After the wedding, I couldn't bear to see the two of them together. I moved away in the hopes I'd find my own true love. When that didn't happen, I threw myself into work and became a foster mother for a while."

"That was good of you," Tiffany said.

"It felt like the right thing to do. It helped some, but my family didn't understand. I made fewer and fewer trips home. In time, it was easier to stay away than endure the pity that everyone gave me." Laura dusted her hands as if shaking off the past and faced Tiffany. "You're the perfect combination of your parents. Thankfully, you inherited the Jackson nose and not the Devereux beak."

Tiffany laughed at the odd compliment, but she wasn't quite ready to let the story go. Instead of responding, she grabbed a cookie and took a bite. Her aunt's story was unlike anything she had imagined. She always thought her parents were madly in love, but now she wondered if that had truly been the case.

Finally, Tiffany said, "Can I ask you something?"

"Of course. All my skeletons are out of the closet."

"Did my dad really love my mom, or did he settle for her because you broke up with him?" Tiffany held her breath as she waited for the answer.

Laura took both of Tiffany's hands in hers and smiled the saddest smile Tiffany had ever seen. "Sweet girl, your dad loved your mother very much. He may have liked me, but your mother stole his heart. She was the reason he got up every morning, put on that uniform, and faced the dangers of his job. She was his sunshine and fresh air, his love and laughter. She was his sanctuary. She was his entire world."

Even though Tiffany was relieved to hear that, she felt saddened by her aunt's hurt expression. It appeared that Laura's heart was breaking all over again.

Grace

"Making these ahead of time was a great idea," Grace said, taking the trays of canapés out of the refrigerator and setting them on the marble island in the middle of the kitchen. "Did you and Dean enjoy your time away this afternoon?"

"We did," Charlotte said as she uncorked a bottle of wine for hospitality hour. "We ended up at the barbecue festival."

Grace glanced up from her task. "Spencer and I were there too, but we didn't see you. If I'd known that's where you were going, we could have had lunch together."

"It was a spur-of-the-moment decision," Charlotte said.

"I understand," Grace said. "But between everyone's hectic schedules, we rarely get a chance for the four of us to spend time together."

"I know," Charlotte said. "I wish I could say with the holidays approaching we'd get more time, but we'll be even busier than ever. Maybe after the first of the year, we can shut down for a week, and the four of us can go on a short vacation. Wouldn't that be great?"

"It certainly would."

Charlotte handed her a glass of chardonnay. "For now, let's take a moment and toast to a nice day."

Grace accepted the glass and touched the edge of Charlotte's with hers. "And to many more."

"Hello, my dears." Winnie sailed into the kitchen with rosy cheeks and bright eyes. She wore a green silk blouse and cream-colored slacks.

"You look fabulous," Grace said. She regarded her own charcoal-gray pants and burgundy shirt. Her outfit wasn't nearly as dressy as her aunt's, but it was suitable for the evening. Likewise, Charlotte wore crisp black cotton pants paired with a peach-colored knit shirt.

"Thank you," Winnie said. "What are we toasting?"

"We were expressing our thanks for the wonderful afternoon you made possible today," Charlotte answered. "So, I guess we were toasting to you."

"In that case, pour me a glass, and I'll join you," Winnie said. "Then I'll go say hello to everyone, but I can only stay for a minute."

"That's right," Grace said. "It's Tuesday. Shouldn't you be on your way to Spool & Thread for your Busy Bees meeting?"

"Not tonight," Winnie answered. "I'm breaking with tradition."

"Where are you off to?" Grace asked. It wasn't unusual for Winnie to pop in and attend to their guests during the nightly hospitality hour. However, Winnie loved her time with her quilting group, so for her to miss a meeting surprised Grace.

"Your uncle is taking me out to dinner," Winnie said. "We're going to try a new restaurant he heard about."

"Here in town?" Charlotte handed her aunt a wineglass. "I haven't heard or seen anything."

"Oh no," Winnie said. "It's over in Summerville."

Grace checked the calendar hanging on the corkboard. Nothing was noted for today. "I didn't mix up my dates, did I? It's not your birthday or anniversary."

Winnie smiled and patted her hand. "No, you're safe. Gus wanted to do something special for me, so I'm letting him."

Charlotte loaded the wine bottles onto a tray and sighed. "I hope that if Dean and I are still together decades from now, he'll continue doing romantic things like that for me."

"Oh, has he said something?" Winnie asked.

"No, it's too soon," Charlotte said. "I'm only saying it would be wonderful to have that kind of long-term relationship like the two of you." She hoisted the tray and nodded toward the canapés. "Shall we get everything set up on the veranda before the guests arrive?"

Before Grace could respond, Charlotte was out the kitchen door and gone.

Grace glanced at her aunt and shrugged.

"Do you think there's trouble in paradise?" Winnie asked.

"No, Charlotte said she enjoyed her day with Dean." Grace frowned. "She seems a little restless lately. Maybe she's ready for a bigger commitment, but he's not. You know Charlotte isn't always the most patient person."

"That's true." Winnie took one of the trays and smiled. "Shall we go see how everyone else's day went?"

Grace and Winnie joined Charlotte on the veranda. They had just finished lighting the candles and setting out the wine, canapés, and glasses when Winston bounded over to them. He barked and plopped down at Grace's feet.

"I think he's telling us that someone is on their way downstairs," Grace said to her sister and aunt. "Good job, Winston."

"I'll turn on the music," Charlotte said, then slipped away.

Ryan and Melinda walked onto the veranda. Both appeared relaxed, a bit sun-kissed, and happy. It was nice to see her guests smiling, but Grace couldn't help worrying at the same time. She knew from her early days as a supposed widow how desperate she'd been at times to fill the void her husband had left behind. She didn't want to see either Ryan or Melinda get hurt. At the same time, it wasn't any of her business.

Ryan walked over to where the wine was set up and started talking to Winnie.

Melinda made a beeline for Grace.

"How was your day at the festival?" Grace asked.

"Surprisingly fun," Melinda replied.

"You thought it would be boring?"

"No, not at all. I love going to town festivals and events, but I was afraid I'd embarrass myself by dropping food on my clothes. Then I did something worse—I upended my plate on Ryan. But he simply laughed it off."

"I can see why that would be a twist on your expectations," Grace said. "Most people—me included—would have been ready to go home and change."

"I'm right there with you," Melinda said. "I couldn't have walked around with a big stain on my pants, and you know they had to be at least damp from where he cleaned it off. But he didn't want to cut our day short. I find that extremely sweet and thoughtful. A rare quality these days."

"That's Ryan for you. He's the type of person who will always put others before himself." Grace had seen him do that with his wife time and time again. Not that Ryan appeared to mind. In fact, it seemed to make him happy to see others taken care of. She couldn't help but wonder if anyone put Ryan first.

"That's good to know," Melinda said. "My mom is a caregiver like that, but it's not exactly my strong suit."

"So we can rule out nursing as a new career for you?" Grace asked as they walked over and leaned against the veranda railing.

"Absolutely."

Grace laughed. "There's nothing wrong with knowing your strengths and weaknesses. That's how I ended up here, running an inn with my sister."

"Tell me more about how that happened."

"I was tired of long workweeks and not having enough time for my son or myself," Grace explained. "I was burned out on the corporate world. It was time to find something else that brought me joy."

"And taking care of a bunch of strangers in your house brings you joy?" Melinda asked.

Grace couldn't help but smile at the sound of incredibility in Melinda's voice. The woman was certainly not a caretaker by nature. "Surprisingly, yes."

"You definitely have a gift for being an innkeeper and making people happy," Melinda said. "You pamper your guests and make them feel at home, and you make it look easy. It's hard to start over when all the careers with real potential require going back to school. It's not something I want to do in my midforties."

"I understand. The idea of sitting in a room where I'd basically be the class mom wasn't appealing to me either," Grace admitted. "But don't forget that you can enroll in online classes. You'd be just another name on the roster then."

"That's true."

"It's never too late to start over," Grace said. "Life is too short to work at a job you don't enjoy. Don't settle. Find something you love. You're great at organization. I love the party spreadsheet you made for me today."

Melinda waved off the compliment. "Oh, that was nothing."

"Well, it's really useful to both me and Charlotte. I'm sorry you're leaving before the party. I wish you could see how much it's helped us."

"What's helping?" Tiffany, who was holding a content Winston, asked from behind Grace.

"A simple spreadsheet I made Grace this morning," Melinda answered. "It was no big deal."

"She's being modest." Grace moved over to open up the conversation to include Tiffany. "Charlotte and I have been so busy that we've had trouble keeping track of who has done what for a surprise party we're hosting this weekend. But thanks to Melinda, we've got it all covered now."

"I love planning parties," Tiffany said. "If there's anything I can do to help, let me know. However, I must warn you that my cooking skills are pretty basic."

"I appreciate the offer, but you're our guest, and you have more important things to do," Grace said. "But I could use your opinion. What do you think of a flashback to the eighties theme party?"

"Personally, that sounds great to me," Melinda said.

"I have to agree," Tiffany said. "I know it's before my time, but I love the music and all those bright colors. How can you go wrong?"

"That's what I was thinking too," Grace said. "How are things coming with your family reunion?" She hoped Tiffany's aunt had been welcoming, although it must have been a tremendous shock to the woman to hear of her sister's passing, and that could have colored her feelings at the time.

"I'm not sure," Tiffany admitted. "My aunt didn't slam the door in my face, but she didn't exactly ask me to keep coming over. I did find out why she and my mom stopped talking."

Tiffany filled them in on the cause of the rift between the two sisters. Grace couldn't imagine going years without ever talking to Charlotte, much less decades.

"But did she tell you to stay away?" Melinda asked.

Tiffany shook her head. "We talked, and she's been kind. I just feel like I'm bothering her, and maybe she wishes I'd go away and leave her alone. I probably should. I could enjoy the rest of my time under that big old magnolia out there with a good book. Or go explore the town."

Charlotte walked over with a bottle of wine and offered the group refills. "I couldn't help but overhear, Tiffany. I don't mean to intrude, but I'm an aunt and I have to say, I can't imagine not loving my nephew, Jake. Even if I was mad at Grace, I'd still want Jake in my life."

"Thank you," Tiffany said.

"Give her time," Charlotte advised. "Losing her sister has to be really hard on her." She glanced at Grace with tears glistening in the corners of her eyes.

Grace slipped her arm around her sister and smiled. "Yes, I can't even imagine what your aunt is going through right now, but I'm sure spending time with you is helping to heal old wounds and get her through new ones."

"Thank you both so much," Tiffany said. "I wish I could find that necklace. It clearly meant a lot to both my mom and aunt."

"We'll keep searching for it." Grace gestured to Charlotte, and they went inside where they could talk in private.

Winnie joined them. "Is everything all right?" She studied Grace. "You seem upset."

Grace didn't want to worry them, but she was concerned. "Tiffany had a necklace for her aunt that's gone missing, and the window screen in her room was torn. Other things have also disappeared, like the key to the shed."

"Do you think someone broke in?" Winnie asked.

Grace considered the possibility. They'd never had anyone break in before. They'd had unscrupulous guests like her ex-husband, Hank. She still had trouble processing that he'd faked his death and lived for years in Europe as a thief, stealing credit cards and identities, before coming back and getting arrested right in the middle of her foyer.

"I don't believe anyone broke in," Grace said. "Tiffany's necklace is the only thing of real value that's missing. The lock is still on the shed, so unless the person opened the shed and hauled out the kayaks, everything of value is still inside."

"What else is missing?" Winnie asked.

"My thimble," Grace said.

"A measuring spoon," Charlotte said.

Winnie frowned. "Why would someone steal a thimble and a measuring spoon?"

"None of this makes sense," Grace said. "We would have noticed a stranger coming into the inn. One of us is always here. We've simply been very busy, and clearly, we're misplacing items."

But Grace wasn't so sure that was the full truth. The mansion was big. How hard would it be for someone to slip in through the back door when she and Charlotte were upstairs cleaning rooms? There were countless hiding places in the old home. Before she worried Charlotte and Winnie any more than she already had, she'd complete a household inventory. She wouldn't mention it again unless she found something else missing.

But at that point she was going to call Spencer for backup.

13

Melinda

It was another beautiful morning in Magnolia Harbor, one full of promise for anyone on a normal vacation, but Melinda wasn't one of those people. After checking her e-mail and getting yet another job application rejection, she was tempted to spend the day in her room. But the smell of freshly brewed coffee and something with cinnamon, butter, and bacon lured her out of bed.

Thank goodness, because as tempting as sulking had been, Melinda was also starving. Plus, during breakfast Tiffany suggested they spend the morning exploring the area together. In other words, having some actual fun.

After finishing their food, Melinda and Tiffany jumped into Melinda's car and took off.

As they cruised down the back roads of South Carolina, slipping into one cute little town after another, the two of them got to know each other better.

When they started talking about their work, Melinda asked Tiffany if she had any ideas about a new career. Yesterday Tiffany had admitted that she wasn't looking forward to returning to her position as a software programmer.

"No, and I don't know what else to do," Tiffany answered. "It's what my degree is in and all I've really done, except for a stint as a waitress, and that's not an option."

Melinda glanced over at her passenger. "Why not?"

Tiffany's cheeks grew pink. "Let's just say my skills do not extend to balancing heavy trays above my head."

"Did you break a few dishes?"

"More than a few," Tiffany replied. "The owner said if I broke any more, he wouldn't be able to open the next day. I did better as a hostess, but it brings back embarrassing memories that I'd rather not revisit."

"It's strange how we're in similar boats and both ended up in Magnolia Harbor," Melinda remarked.

"It must be fate," Tiffany said.

"Maybe fate thinks we can help each other." Melinda flashed her a smile as she slowed down to make a left-hand turn. "What about some other kind of computer job? Are you good at graphic design?"

"I don't know. I've never tried, but what would I do with it?"

"You could start your own business," Melinda suggested. "Design and create signage for businesses or menus for restaurants, book covers, or programs for theaters."

"That sounds interesting, but I'd still be stuck indoors all the time like I am now," Tiffany said. "I'd like to find something that gets me out of the building and around people. I'm so tired of staring at a cubicle wall all day long."

Melinda completely understood. Her job as an accountant had left her locked in her office for hours on end with only her computer and a bunch of numbers for company. "What about being a nanny? Are you good with kids?"

Tiffany paused as if considering the question. Then her expression became comical—a mixture of curiosity and terror. "I used to babysit when I was a teen, but I've never thought about being a nanny. It does have some nice perks like not being stuck indoors all the time."

"Yep, you'd actually be required to go outside when it's nice."

"I might have to give that idea some deeper reflection." Tiffany settled back in her seat, a small smile relaxing her features. "Now, what about you? Have you thought about being a nanny?"

Melinda chuckled. "No. I don't have any experience with kids."

"You could go back to school and become a hairstylist," Tiffany said. "You'd be around people all day then."

"True, but I don't think I want to return to school. Not at my age."

Tiffany threw out a few more ideas, some that Melinda had already considered and discarded. Others, such as becoming a children's party clown, made them both laugh. Melinda was pretty sure that was way outside her skill set.

"There's a party planning store," Tiffany said, pointing. "Let's stop and see if we can get ideas for the surprise party Grace is planning."

Melinda parked her car, and the two of them entered the store. They browsed the aisles until they came to one containing neon party props. There were balloons, confetti, and noisemakers. The costumes for men and women featured lots of headbands, leg warmers, and brightly colored T-shirts. There was even a life-size cutout of a famous pop duo from the eighties.

Tiffany asked one of the sales clerks if she'd take their picture and then pulled Melinda behind the giant cardboard stand.

"I'll send it to you," Tiffany promised. "It'll be our vacation souvenir."

Melinda laughed.

After the clerk took the picture, they continued to peruse the merchandise. The store had everything Grace would need, but Melinda's favorite was the rack of CDs.

"Check out this collection. It's like every great song from the eighties." Melinda picked up one case and scanned the song list. "I think I'll grab a couple of them and give one to Grace. I'd like to thank her for her kindness and advice."

"That's a good idea," Tiffany said. "I'm sure she'll appreciate it."

After paying for the CDs, Melinda and Tiffany hopped into the car and headed back to the inn. The return trip was much shorter as they took the direct route rather than continuing with the scenic route.

As she pulled into the inn's drive, Melinda asked, "What are your plans for this afternoon?"

"I'm going to visit my aunt again," Tiffany said. "I want to get to know her better. But I feel terrible about the lost necklace. I hate not being able to honor my mom's last wish."

"I'm betting her real wish was to bring you and your aunt together." Melinda parked the car and grabbed the bag of CDs. "I had a great time. Thank you for getting me out of my funk."

"I did too," Tiffany said. "If we have a chance, we should do something else together."

They walked to the front porch and climbed the steps.

"Are you going to give that to Grace now?" Tiffany asked as she opened the door.

Melinda followed her friend into the foyer. "If she's around."

"If who's around?" Grace popped up from behind the reception desk, a smear of dirt across her cheek.

"You." Melinda removed one of the CDs from the bag. "Going by the smudge on your cheek, I'm guessing you're still searching for your lost key."

Grace chuckled and rubbed at the spot. "That and doing some reorganizing. What's this?" She picked up the CD and flipped it over. "This takes me back. I haven't heard some of these songs in years."

"We ran across a party store," Melinda said. "They have everything you could possibly need for the surprise party. But that CD is for you. I wanted to thank you for lending me your ear and your shoulder to cry on."

"This is so sweet and totally unnecessary," Grace said.

Melinda's heart sank. Grace hated the gift.

Grace must have picked up on her sudden mood change, because she reached out and hugged her. "What I mean is, I love the gift, but my friendship and advice are always free of charge."

The three chatted for a few minutes about the surprise party. Tiffany excused herself to run up to her room before she went to her aunt's.

Melinda left Grace to her chores and drove into town. Her job search was taking much longer than she'd imagined, and she wondered how she would fill her time until she landed a new position. When she got home, she'd investigate volunteer opportunities. Maybe she could become a tour guide or a docent at one of the historic homes in her area. Or perhaps she'd take Ryan up on his job offer. It would keep her busy, reduce the dent in her savings, and give her an excuse to stay in touch with him.

In the meantime, Melinda stopped at Spool & Thread to discover a new hobby. As she perused the piles of material and spools of thread, her mood fell. With each passing day and no promising job leads, she realized that she had nothing. She'd been so devoted to work that she'd forgotten how to have a good time.

"How nice to see you here."

A friendly voice pulled Melinda out of her musings. When she glanced up, it was into the smiling eyes of Winnie.

"Have you come to learn to quilt after all?" Winnie asked.

"Could you suggest something else?" Melinda said. "Preferably something a little smaller and less intimidating."

"Hmm." Winnie scanned the shop. A moment later, her whole face lit up. "Come with me."

Melinda followed her to an aisle in the back. "What's this?"

"Embroidery," Winnie said. "You use small stitches to create beautiful pictures that you can then make into other things like pillows, table runners, or even embellishments on shirts or pants."

"That sounds useful." Melinda hoped she would enjoy it. She wanted to add some fun into her life as well as fill the empty hours.

"Here, this is a great starter set," Winnie said, removing a box from the shelf and handing it to Melinda. "It's got everything you'll need."

Melinda took the kit. It was for a magnolia tree, and the kit suggested framing it. Perfect. It was rated for ages eight and up. Even better—that meant it was easy.

She thanked Winnie, paid for the kit, and stepped out into the sunshine, feeling a little less weighed down. It wouldn't break her bank account, but it would give her something else to focus on.

Melinda turned toward the Dragonfly Coffee Shop and ran smack-dab into a solid chest. "I'm so sorry . . . Oh, Ryan, it's you."

"Does that mean you're no longer sorry?" he teased.

"Not at all," she said. "What are you doing here? I thought you had a meeting with your client all day."

"We wrapped up early," Ryan said. "Would you like to go antiquing with me? I need to pick up a few items, and it's always more pleasant with a friend."

A small thrill zinged through her. "I'd love to. What are you searching for?"

"First, how about some lunch?" he asked.

"Sounds good. I was going to grab a snack, but I could go for something more substantial. Let me drop this in my car." Melinda went to her car, popped the trunk, and placed the small bag inside.

They left her car where it was, and Ryan drove them to Cappy's pizza parlor. They discovered a shared love of sausage-and-mushroom deep-dish pizza. Melinda told him about her sightseeing trip with Tiffany that morning. Ryan filled her in on his earlier meeting and his client's request for antique drawer pulls.

"Speaking of work, my job offer still stands," Ryan said. "I don't want you to feel any pressure to take it, but I also want you to know I meant it when I asked."

Melinda smiled. It was clear his offer was sincere, but he wasn't being pushy, which would have made the prospect much less pleasant for her.

She couldn't deny that she was tempted to accept the job, but she was also afraid to do so. It would be falling back into her comfort zone, which would be the easy path but also the less fulfilling one. Then there was the friendship building between her and Ryan. With each minute spent in his company, she found herself hoping it might grow into something more.

If she wasn't mistaken, he did too.

After a delicious lunch, they drove out of Magnolia Harbor and into the rural landscape.

Melinda enjoyed Ryan's company more and more. He was quiet but interesting and considerate. He let her pick the radio station, and he didn't complain when she sang imperfectly. As they talked about life in general, she discovered they had even more things in common.

About an hour later, they pulled into a dirt parking lot and stopped in front of a one-story building that had seen better days. Melinda imagined that the faded and chipped paint had once been red. Now it was barely pink. The roof was missing some shingles, and it appeared swaybacked in places.

"Are you sure it's safe to go inside?" she asked.

"Probably," Ryan said as he eyed the building. "Hopefully."

"That's not very reassuring."

"Actually, it's looking a little better than it did last year when I was here. I think they've had some work done." He climbed out of the car and came around to open her door.

If this was an improvement, she was glad she hadn't seen it before.

When they entered the store, an elderly gentleman with snow-white hair that stuck out in every direction greeted them. "If you need any help, give me a holler."

"Thanks," Ryan said as he started to browse.

"Do you know much about antiques?" Melinda asked.

"Not really," Ryan admitted.

"Then how do you know what to buy or if you're getting a good deal?" She picked up a chipped porcelain pitcher, wondering who would want something that was broken, then set it down.

"I go with my gut. If I like something and feel the asking price is reasonable, I purchase it." Ryan walked around the piles of old items scattered throughout the building.

Melinda followed. She examined a few things that caught her eye, such as an old brooch and a glass bowl that she thought her mom might appreciate, but eventually she put them all back. She had no idea if the prices were right. The place felt like an indoor yard sale, but it was interesting perusing the items and speculating about the people who had owned them.

"Do you see anything you like?" he asked, glancing down at the crystal heart-shaped bowl that her hand was resting on.

Melinda casually slipped her hand into her pocket. "There are a lot of fascinating pieces in here, but I wouldn't know what's worth taking home."

Ryan met her eyes and smiled. "Sometimes you have to take a chance and follow your heart."

Melinda didn't know how to respond. Was he talking about her choosing an antique, his job offer, or something else? The way he'd smiled at her had felt like a whole lot of something else. Something that sent butterflies fluttering in her stomach.

He picked up the glass bowl and continued strolling through the store, peering into bins and piles and drawers.

An idea started to form in Melinda's mind.

"These are perfect," Ryan declared, holding up a couple of old drawer pulls.

They appeared a bit tarnished and dull to Melinda, but she was sure with a little work they'd be as good as new again.

"Are you ready to go?" he asked.

"Yes, I found what I needed here," she said.

Ryan noticed her empty hands and gave her a puzzled glance.

Melinda didn't explain. She simply grinned and moved past him toward the elderly gentleman at the counter.

Ryan didn't say anything as he followed. He set the drawer pulls on the counter and opened his wallet.

Melinda's gaze landed on a picture of Ryan and a woman in his wallet. She froze. "Who's that?"

Ryan gently traced his finger along the woman's hair. "Beth."

Melinda studied the picture more closely. She couldn't believe it. Beth could have been her twin.

She wasn't the only one who noticed the resemblance. The clerk leaned forward and grunted. "She looks like you," he said to Melinda.

She was too stunned to respond.

The clerk gave Ryan the total for his purchases and slid the drawer pulls into a bag.

After Ryan paid, the clerk handed him the bag and thanked him.

Ryan ushered Melinda out to the car.

When they were seated, he gave her the crystal heart-shaped bowl. "I hope you don't mind. I saw you admiring this."

"Thank you," Melinda said. "That's so sweet. I forgot you picked it up, and I didn't even notice it on the counter." She grinned. "Very sneaky."

As they drove to Magnolia Harbor, they fell into silence.

But Melinda was locked in an internal battle. She knew he'd been widowed, but she didn't know that she was the woman's doppelgänger. How could Ryan really be interested in her when every time he gazed at her face, he saw his dead wife? Clearly, Melinda was just a replacement for Beth.

So much for her big idea of planning a date for the two of them tonight. Suddenly Melinda had a headache. She had been such a fool to let herself start falling for Ryan. It was a good thing she hadn't accepted his job offer. That would have made things even more awkward.

When they arrived at her car in downtown Magnolia Harbor, Ryan parked and came around to open her door. Always the gentleman.

"Will I see you in a bit for wine and appetizers?" he asked with a smile.

Melinda pressed her fingers to her temple. "I've got a headache coming on, so I think I'll call it an early night."

Ryan's gaze dropped to the heart-shaped bowl in her hands, his smile gone, but he nodded. "I hope you change your mind."

As she watched him drive away, she whispered to the wind, "If only it were that easy."

14

Tiffany

After her morning excursion with Melinda, Tiffany's mood was as bright as the afternoon sun. Her feet practically danced over the ground as she hurried to her aunt's door, which stood open. Inside the house, soft music played, and Laura sang along. Tiffany gave the screen door a couple of solid knocks to be heard over the din and waited.

"Come on in," Laura called out. "I'm in the kitchen."

Tiffany stepped inside the house for the very first time and glanced around. Laura kept a tidy home, and she certainly didn't believe in clutter. There were no knickknacks lining shelves and collecting dust. There were no throw pillows or afghans draped over chairs or the sofa. No discarded shoes or jackets lying about.

The only personal effects in the living room were lots of books, all neatly lined up on built-in shelves, and a few picture frames gracing one end of the fireplace mantel. The other end held two candles, possibly in case of a power outage.

Normally, Tiffany wouldn't snoop through someone else's belongings, but one of the pictures caught her attention. It was of two young girls, identical in so many ways yet so very different.

Mom.

She couldn't help but pick up the frame and examine the photo. The sisters gazed at the camera with carefree grins. Their heads were bent together, and they gave each other bunny ears.

If only they hadn't fallen in love with the same man. If only her mom had seen the doctor sooner.

Tiffany sighed. She could play the if-only game all day, but it wouldn't change the past.

Before she set the frame back, she pulled her cell phone out and snapped a picture of the photo. If nothing else, at least she would have this memory to treasure.

Tiffany poked her head into the spotless kitchen with white cabinets and yellow accents. The scent of apples and cinnamon wafted through the air. "It smells great in here."

Her aunt stood in front of the stove. "It's about time you got here," she chided.

Tiffany stood up straight, a hopeful smile chasing away the blues her if-only game had brought on. They hadn't made plans for Tiffany to return today, so Laura's comment surprised and pleased her. Maybe they were making progress after all.

"Sorry," Tiffany said, stepping into the room. "I got waylaid looking at a picture on the mantel."

"Stir that pot, and don't let it burn." Laura thrust an apron and a wooden spoon into her hands. "I expected you'd be on my doorstep first thing this morning."

Tiffany stirred the pot, making sure nothing was sticking, before turning to her aunt. "I'm sorry. Did I forget that we'd made plans?"

"Did we make plans the other times you showed up?" Laura asked. She sat down at the table and started peeling pears.

"No. If I'm interrupting, I can leave. I don't want to overstay my welcome."

"Did I ask you to leave? Keep stirring."

"Is everything okay? You seem upset." *Please, Lord, don't let her be sick too.*

"I'm just tired," Laura replied, her tone slightly apologetic. "I overdid it in the yard yesterday, and these old bones and muscles complained last night."

"I'm sorry to hear that."

"Now, how was your morning?" her aunt asked, changing the subject. "Did you get lost talking to that guy of yours?"

Tiffany laughed and faced the stove. Thankfully, she could blame the heat for her flushed cheeks. "No, Chris is busy getting ready for his deployment, and I haven't had a chance to talk to him much lately. I went exploring with one of the other guests this morning."

"Are you ready to pack up and move to my neck of the woods?" Laura asked.

Her aunt's tone was casual, teasing, yet Tiffany picked up the undercurrents. Or maybe that was wishful thinking on her part.

"If I wasn't so fond of city convenience, sure," Tiffany replied. "Then there's that whole long-distance love affair factor. It's hard enough on us with Chris deploying."

"I understand," Laura said.

Tiffany decided to take a chance. "I'm hoping this week won't be the last you and I see of each other, though."

"Family is always welcome at my door."

Except for my parents, Tiffany thought. "You're more than welcome to visit me too. I'd love for you to meet Chris."

"Keep stirring." Laura continued peeling, slicing, and coring the pears.

The way her aunt ignored her invitation hurt, but Tiffany understood. The idea of returning to Georgia probably brought too much pain with it.

"What am I making anyway?" Tiffany asked.

"Apple butter, if you don't burn it, and then we're going to can cinnamon pears. I'm also in the mood for chocolate cake." Laura took the wooden spoon from her, clucking at the splatters Tiffany had already managed to get on her apron.

After testing the cooked apples, Laura set the pot aside to cool and handed Tiffany a bag of flour. "Why don't you start on the cake? I'm not sure it's safe to give you a knife."

That was probably true. Tiffany never claimed to be a gourmet chef. She had a few basic go-to recipes. Very basic recipes. Stuff she'd learned to make as a kid—grilled cheese sandwiches, omelets, protein smoothies, and garlic-lemon grilled chicken—but she'd never ventured into the world of baking or expanding her recipe index.

As soon as Tiffany dropped the bag on the counter, a puff of flour shot up into her face. She sighed. That was exactly why she stayed out of the baking arena.

Laura lifted a brow, but she didn't say anything, other than to point out the recipe card on the shelf and where various items like bowls and the mixer were located.

Tiffany scooped, measured, and stirred. She crushed a couple of eggs while cracking them, and she was unable to salvage them.

Still, Laura said nothing. She simply sat there, peeling, slicing, and coring her pears.

Tiffany placed the hand mixer into the bowl and took a deep breath. This part never went well for her.

"Relax," Laura said. "It's not going to bite."

Tiffany turned the mixer on low, slowly increasing the speed as the dry ingredients blended with the wet until a nice, smooth batter formed. Excited to sample her creation—every cook had to taste the batter first, right?—she lifted the mixer out and screamed as chocolate went flying.

Laura jumped out of her chair, lunged for the mixer, and switched it off.

But it was too late. Her once immaculate kitchen was streaked with chocolate. It was on the counter and the cupboard doors. It was on the floor and the refrigerator that sat five feet from where Tiffany stood. It was on the window panes. It was on Tiffany's face—her cheeks, her eyelids, her lips—but it tasted great.

Laura shook her head, but she didn't say a word.

"I'm so sorry." Tiffany went to set the mixer on the counter. She was so busy scanning the mess she'd made that she didn't see a china cup sitting on the counter until she knocked it over with the mixer. The cup crashed to the floor, shattering into dozens of tiny pieces. Sort of like her life.

"Don't move," Laura commanded.

"Let me get that," Tiffany said. "It's all my fault."

"Don't move," her aunt repeated. "I don't want you to get cut."

Tiffany stood helplessly as she watched her aunt take care of the mess she'd made. Before she'd arrived, Laura's kitchen had been orderly, like her life before Tiffany had disrupted it. She should clean up the rest of the disaster and leave, so Laura could get back to her normal life.

As Tiffany reached for a paper towel, she heard the distinctive sound of sniffling. She bent down and reached for her aunt's hands. "Did you cut yourself? You should have let me clean it up."

"I'm fine," Laura answered. "Go sit down before I don't have a kitchen left."

Tiffany straightened, but she didn't sit down. "Please tell me that cup wasn't an antique or a family heirloom."

"No, it was neither. It was a pretty thing I picked up at a yard sale." Laura dumped the broken shards into the trash and washed her hands. "Have a seat, and I'll handle the rest."

"I'm not a complete disaster in the kitchen," Tiffany said, sitting down at the table. "I can clean."

"Better safe than sorry." Laura started wiping down the counters, cupboards, and appliances. "I actually want to eat that cake."

Tiffany chuckled. Her aunt had a point. "If the cup wasn't special, why were you crying?"

Laura stopped cleaning long enough to drop a quick, unexpected kiss onto the top of Tiffany's head. "Happy tears. Your mom and I used to make jams, can, and bake together."

"My mom?" Tiffany snorted. "Compared to her, I'm a baking prodigy. If it wasn't for my dad, I would have lived on grilled cheese and cereal." She smiled at a lost memory. "Mom made the worst jam ever. She tried, but it was awful. It was runny and so sweet that it hurt your teeth."

"Even so, I'll bet you ate it every time she made it," Laura said as she finished tidying up the kitchen.

"I did, and I told her I loved it."

"Good girl." Laura laughed. "Between the mess Donna would make and the taste, we finally had to hide her jars. Then I'd bring up the ones Mama or I made, and we'd tell her they were hers."

"You lied?" Tiffany asked.

"She meant well. Like you." Laura poured two glasses of sweet tea and gave one to Tiffany. "Tell me more about this job of yours and your guy. Are you looking forward to getting back to your life soon?"

Tiffany was taken aback.

"What is it?" Laura asked.

There was such a familiar tenderness in her voice that all Tiffany's resolutions to keep her visit light went right out the window. Before she knew it, she was spilling her grief and fear to her aunt. "I can't return to my old life. I want to quit my job, Chris is deploying, and Mom is gone forever. There's no going back. I have to figure out how to move forward, and I don't know if I'm strong enough to face it all alone."

"You'd be surprised at how strong you can be when forced with no other choice," Laura said gently. "And you're not alone. I'm only a phone call away."

"Thank you," Tiffany said, touched by her aunt's words. "That means a lot. Navigating my relationship with Chris is hard enough, but trying to figure out how to do it long-distance, even temporarily, is going to be hard."

"Can you call each other?" Laura asked. "Or e-mail or video chat?"

"We'll definitely try, although the time difference will make it difficult," Tiffany answered. "But I guess if my parents could deal with Mom working evenings and Dad working days, Chris and I can get through this too."

Laura retrieved a cake pan from the cupboard and practically slammed it onto the counter. For a moment, she didn't move or say anything.

Startled, Tiffany jumped. She didn't know what to do.

"Keep reminding yourself that this separation from Chris is only temporary," Laura said. "Remember that he doesn't want to be away from you any more than you want him gone. Before you know it, he'll be home."

Tiffany nodded.

"Now, tell me about wanting to change jobs."

"I feel lost there too," Tiffany admitted. "I'm doing what I went to school for, so I don't know what else to do." Trying to lighten the mood, she added, "One of the other guests at the inn suggested that I become a nanny."

"If you like kids, you could also try tutoring," Laura suggested. "Or if you're willing to go back to school, you could become a teacher."

"That's true," Tiffany mused. "Mom often said that if she hadn't become a nurse, she would have wanted to be a teacher. And after a hard day at work, Dad often said he was going to quit and be a gym teacher."

"Of course, there are plenty of other jobs where you can help people, like hospitality and customer service," Laura said as if Tiffany hadn't spoken.

Tiffany got it—her parents were still a sore topic of conversation, but it was impossible to talk about her life and her past without mentioning them. They'd been a close family. Sunday dinners together. Holidays spent gathered in the living room, carrying out traditions. She regularly dropped by their house to say hello and picked up the phone to tell them about her day.

How could Tiffany share her past with her aunt and leave out the most important parts—the people who had raised her, loved her, and shaped her into the person she was now? It was like making a chocolate cake and leaving out the cocoa powder.

But she had to try. It was the only way to build a relationship with Laura, her last living relative.

Melinda

When Melinda arrived at the inn, she hoped to escape to her suite without running into anyone. Her head hurt, and she didn't think she could face everyone and pretend things were okay. She still couldn't believe the striking resemblance between her and Ryan's late wife. It was eerie.

As soon as she walked through the front door, the bell jingled, and Winston bounded over with ecstatic barking.

She stopped to give him some love.

"Oh good, you're back," Charlotte said, entering the room. She wore black pants and a crisp white blouse. "Tiffany and Ryan are here too, and I'm about to bring out this evening's appetizers."

"You're looking quite formal tonight," Melinda commented.

"I'm going over to The Tidewater to lend a hand because they're short-staffed in the kitchen," Charlotte explained. "But don't worry. I've already got your snacks ready to go. I made a delicious pear, brie, and balsamic bruschetta, and I have the perfect wine to go with it."

"That sounds wonderful," Melinda said.

Charlotte smiled. "It's just what you need after a day of sightseeing and shopping."

Melinda winced. "Actually, I've got a terrible headache. I think I'm going to skip the hospitality hour and rest in my room."

Charlotte's easy smile disappeared, replaced by concern. "How about if I make you a pot of chamomile tea and bring it up? Not only will it ease your headache, but it'll help you sleep better."

Melinda reached out and squeezed Charlotte's hand. "That would be lovely. Thank you for being so kind."

"You're welcome," Charlotte said. "Is everything else all right? You seem sad."

"It's nothing that a good night's sleep won't cure," Melinda assured her.

Charlotte nodded and promised to bring up the tea shortly.

Melinda gave Winston one last ear scratch before she ascended the stairs and retreated to her room. The first thing she did was head to the bathroom for a cold compress. Then she kicked off her shoes and slipped into a pair of soft yoga pants and her favorite oversize sweatshirt. Both were soft and warm and wrapped her in comfort.

She dropped into the chair closest to the window and gazed out at the lake. As she relaxed, she started feeling better, and her headache began to subside.

The last several months had been an emotional roller coaster. If she didn't make some serious decisions soon, eventually it was going to become a runaway train. Melinda might not have consciously decided to become an accountant, but she'd pretty much been in charge of most everything else in her life . . . until recently. It was time to get back into the driver's seat.

But how?

For some reason, Melinda rummaged in her purse and pulled out the strange little tea tin that Winnie had given her. She turned it over and studied it, barely able to read the label.

"Mint tea," she murmured. "Why did she give me an old and empty tin of mint tea?"

From the few conversations she'd had with Winnie and everything Ryan had said, the woman was as sharp as a tack. What was Melinda missing? She examined the tin again to see if it had been made here in Magnolia Harbor, but she couldn't make out anything else. Most of the label had been worn away years ago.

"Obsessing over the why isn't going to give me any answers," she said out loud to the empty room. "I'll ask Winnie next time I see her, because I know the more I try to figure it out, the more elusive the answer will be. Sort of like the question of what I'll do with my life."

Yet her mind wouldn't let go of the tin. As she watched a couple of boats on the lake, she kept repeating *mint tea* in her head. It had almost become a chant or a mantra. Either way, it was rather soothing. She even felt her eyes start to drift close. Not that she slept. She wasn't so much tired as simply relaxed. After being away from the hustle and bustle of her life in Roswell, the restless feeling that had dogged her since she'd lost her job had finally quieted.

Despite discovering that she was Ryan's late wife's doppelgänger, the past few days had been the best she'd had in months. Melinda wasn't looking forward to her vacation ending and saying goodbye to her new friends.

"I could sell my house and move to Magnolia Harbor, then get a job at the Dragonfly Coffee Shop or the cute little bookstore I saw." She jumped up from the chair and strode to the window. "I could go kayaking on the lake every day. I could also join The Busy Bees and learn how to quilt. There's nothing stopping me."

Except she'd miss her parents and her lovely old Victorian with the wraparound porch that was perfect for holiday decorations. She stared down at the old tea tin still clutched in her grasp. The faded letters swam before her eyes, and a dull thud pressed against her temples again.

Melinda set the tea tin down. All her thinking might have strained her brain, but she had made a decision.

"I may not have solved the mystery of the mint tea, but I do know that I'm done with accounting," she declared, feeling confident, strong, and a bit scared but excited at the same time.

Melinda didn't know what she was going to do for work. That would come next, but she knew she wanted to be around people, not numbers. No more being tied to a desk. She wanted freedom.

A soft knock on the door interrupted her thoughts.

Melinda rushed to the door and opened it. Charlotte stood there with the promised tea.

"I hope I didn't wake you," she said.

"No," Melinda said. "Thank you again."

"My pleasure." Charlotte entered the room and set the tray on the little desk in the corner. In addition to the teapot and a matching cup and saucer, there was a covered plate. "I also brought some appetizers from hospitality hour. You should have a bite to eat too."

"Thanks." Melinda went over and lifted the lid to find chocolate-covered strawberries, pear-and-brie bites, stuffed mushrooms, fruit, cheese, and crackers. She definitely wouldn't need to worry about dinner. "You go above and beyond taking care of your guests."

Charlotte smiled. "That's the idea."

"Everything smells delicious," Melinda said. "So, how's the planning going for the surprise party?"

"It's been a little slow because Grace and I have been so busy lately."

"You should have a dance contest," Melinda suggested. "Or even a best costume contest, so that people really get into the theme."

"I love those ideas," Charlotte said. "Both contests sound like they'd be a blast and a great way to get people involved. I'll run them by Grace, but I think she'll be on board with them too. You've got a knack for planning parties."

"I did my parents' fiftieth anniversary party on my own last year," Melinda said. "Everything is still fresh in my mind."

"That's impressive," Charlotte said, then checked her watch. "I'd better get going. Feel better soon."

"Thank you so much. I'm sure I'll see you at breakfast."

After Charlotte left, Melinda poured herself a cup of the steaming tea, added a dollop of honey, and bit into one of the pear-and-brie bites. If only she could cook like Charlotte, she'd know exactly what to do with her life. As it was, she could cook, but she wasn't a creative chef. That career was off the list.

What she needed was a list so she could spread everything out in front of her—all her pros and cons, her skills and deficits. From there, she could get a better idea of the big picture.

Melinda scooted the food aside and opened her laptop. She started with a list of everything she was good at. The first item was easy. After a couple of decades, she was more than good at accounting. But did she like it still?

No.

She stared at the word *accounting*. It had defined her for so long. Too long. She deleted it.

What now? The question reminded her that she still needed to give Ryan an answer about his job offer.

Could Melinda work for him, even temporarily and part-time, knowing she resembled his late wife? It was kind of weird. More importantly, whom did Ryan see when he looked at Melinda? Did he see her or Beth? Melinda wasn't sure she wanted to know. Or more accurately, she wasn't sure she was brave enough to find out.

It was obvious that she couldn't take the job. She'd have to find something else to do until a permanent solution was found.

But she really liked Ryan.

In the column under skills, she typed: *organization*. In the column under deficits, she typed: *decision-making*.

Because clearly Melinda had a problem making up her mind these days. She never used to be that way. Was that a sign of age creeping up on her? Dementia didn't normally surface in people's forties, but it was certainly possible. And her grandfather had had Alzheimer's disease. She shook her head. It was more likely caused by stress.

In the deficits column, she typed: *overactive imagination*.

Melinda sighed as she scanned the document. There were already more items in the deficit column than the one containing skills.

She concentrated on her strengths. She was skilled at math, she liked people and dogs, and she had an open heart . . .

Maybe that last item should go in the deficit column. After all, if she had guarded her heart more, she wouldn't be feeling the tiniest bit as if Ryan had used her. As much as she liked him, she couldn't help but hear the small voice in her head saying she was only a replacement for Beth. And that hurt.

Melinda shoved all thoughts of Ryan out of her mind as she focused on her list. Thankfully, as she kept working, each column got longer, with the skills column edging out the deficit column.

After a while, she stopped and took stock. Her skills were clearly geared toward working in an office, but she still had more work to do.

She created a new column of things she enjoyed and typed: *be outside*, followed by: *be around people and dogs*.

Melinda smiled as she thought of Winston, her sweet four-legged friend, and made her second firm decision. As soon as she got home, she was visiting the local animal shelter and adopting a dog. Maybe even a cat. And a bird. Perhaps she'd get a goat and open a petting zoo for the local kids. She had enough land. She laughed at the idea, and it felt as if she were laughing away her fear and anxiety.

With each strike of her keyboard, her mood lifted, the pounding at her temples eased, and she once again felt hope.

She could shape her own future.

She only needed some direction and courage.

While her employment future suddenly seemed bright—or at least more promising than it had a week ago—a part of her was still disappointed. She had hoped that she had finally met someone special with Ryan. But she had to be honest. While they had developed a nice friendship, the chances of it going any further were unlikely. Distance didn't affect accounting, but relationships rarely survived the miles.

16

Tiffany

Dark gray clouds blew in from the east as Tiffany sat on the front veranda at the inn with Winston curled up in her lap. She adored the sweet dog and was thankful Grace didn't mind sharing him with her guests, because she really needed his comforting presence.

The day had started out wonderful with her and Melinda's sightseeing outing, but the time with her aunt hadn't gone quite as well as she'd hoped. They had talked and maybe even started to build a connection, but if so, it was loose and fragile. Tiffany was afraid one wrong word, or rather two—her parents—could cause it to unravel quickly. She was also missing Chris and dreading his deployment. And she'd missed talking to Melinda during hospitality hour. They had just met, but the connection between them was instantaneous, natural, and strong.

Everything it should have been with her aunt.

Talking with Melinda had been easy, carefree, and without fear of judgment. Talking with Laura had been like baking a cake. It was simple, but Tiffany felt if she let her guard down, she would miss a step and have a mess on her hands.

Laura pushed Tiffany to talk about herself. But how could she when she had to measure every word and weigh every thought before she spoke? How could she tell her aunt about her life but exclude her parents, especially her mom? They had been so close and shared everything. Well, almost everything. Her mom had kept her twin sister a secret. She had also kept the cancer a secret for weeks before telling Tiffany. But that wasn't the point.

Tiffany wanted Laura to tell her more about Tiffany's mom and grandparents and share stories about her childhood. Not only what life was like for Laura after moving to South Carolina. That was only half of her story. Like life without Tiffany's parents was only half of her story.

Maybe Laura needed more time to process the situation. Or maybe Tiffany was wasting valuable time that she could be spending with Chris before he shipped out. She still hadn't found the missing necklace, and while she was building some kind of bond with her aunt, she didn't know if she would ever forge the family connection she craved.

The front door quietly clicked shut, and Winnie approached.

Tiffany smiled at her, completely charmed by the innkeepers' aunt. "Good evening."

"Do you mind if I join you?" Winnie pointed to the chair next to Tiffany.

"I'd love some company," Tiffany said.

Winston yipped as if in agreement.

"Ryan mentioned that he went fishing this morning with your husband," Tiffany remarked.

"If you can call it fishing when they come home empty-handed." Winnie laughed. "I was looking forward to fresh fish for dinner tonight."

"I'm so stuffed from Charlotte's appetizers that I don't have room for dinner. Your niece is a fabulous cook."

"Yes, she is. Speaking of, I wanted to let you know that Charlotte is out for the evening—she's helping at The Tidewater—and Grace is also out for a little while. If you need anything, let me know, and I'll be happy to help."

"Thanks," Tiffany said.

Winnie started to leave, but she hesitated, as if she wanted to say something but wasn't sure she should.

Tiffany took Winnie's hesitation as an opportunity to keep her talking. "I didn't realize you work at the inn during the evening."

"Officially, I don't work here," Winnie said. "But lending a hand keeps me young and gives my nieces a break once in a while."

"You're all very lucky to have family around." Tiffany dropped her gaze to the dog in her lap and stroked his head. "I knew someday I'd have to say a final goodbye to my parents, but I didn't expect to do it so soon."

"Have you talked with Charlotte?" Winnie asked. "You two are fairly close in age, and she lost her mother too."

"But she wasn't alone," Tiffany said. "She still had you, Grace, and your husband. I don't have any relatives, except for a reluctant aunt who can't stand for me to talk about my parents."

"Actually, I understand that."

Tiffany was shocked. Somehow she couldn't picture this warm, caring woman reacting to anything the way her aunt reacted to the mention of Tiffany's parents. "You do?"

"When my sister, Hazel, died, simply hearing her name made my heart ache even more than it already did." Winnie wiped the tears from her eyes. "Our parents were long gone, so I'd experienced loss before, but nothing prepares you for saying goodbye to a sibling. Your first best friend."

"I never thought about it that way," Tiffany admitted.

"When our parents died, it was awful, of course, but as you said, a child expects to have to say goodbye in time," Winnie continued. "Hazel was my big sister, my protector, my confidant, my teacher, and my best friend. I had never really imagined a world without her."

"She must have thought she was the luckiest person in the world to have had you for a sister," Tiffany murmured.

"That's sweet, but I was the lucky one," Winnie responded. "My grief consumed me for a long time. It ate away at my soul. It filled me with doubt and guilt. We always think we can do more, but the truth is, we have very little control over the matters of life and death. We do the best we can, and then we pray."

Tiffany explained the rift between her mother and aunt. "Do you think my aunt feels guilty for loving my dad? Or for leaving?"

Tiffany didn't want Laura to feel bad for falling in love with him. She knew that people couldn't control their hearts, only their actions. But a little part of her did blame her aunt for leaving and staying away all those years. She understood it was easier for Laura not to see her sister with the man she loved, but she could have kept in touch. Then Tiffany wouldn't have had to be the bearer of bad news. Maybe she would have even had a relationship with Laura while she was growing up.

"I'm sure she does," Winnie answered, "but she's also hurting."

"How did you get over your sister's death?" Tiffany asked, wondering if there was a local support group she could recommend.

"Time helped heal that wound," Winnie said. "I also learned to redirect all the love I had for Hazel and share my memories of her with her daughters."

"Is that what helped Grace and Charlotte? Because if so, I'm out of luck."

Winnie reached over and took one of Tiffany's hands in hers. "No, you're not. You need to give your aunt some time. Don't give up on her. Don't close your heart to her. Give her a chance."

"I've been trying to do that for the past couple of days," Tiffany said. "Every time I mention my parents, she stiffens up."

"If a person is exposed to something enough times, they'll learn to get over their aversion," Winnie said. "Once your aunt gets to know you better, she'll let go of her reluctance. She'll probably even be thankful for your parents' union because now she's not alone. She has a wonderful niece to love."

"Thank you," Tiffany said, fighting back tears. "You have no idea how much I needed to hear that. I've still got a couple of days to break down the wall around my aunt's heart. Even when I get home, I'm not going to stop trying."

"Your mother would be so proud of you." Winnie squeezed her hand and disappeared inside.

Winnie's words gave Tiffany the encouragement she needed to stick around and keep trying to connect with her aunt. They were also a strong reminder that life didn't come with guarantees of happiness and a person had to create their own.

With that in mind, Tiffany pulled her tablet out of her purse and started to search for a new job. Living on the outskirts of a city like Atlanta meant there were numerous pages of job listings. She had to narrow down her search.

One way was to rule out computer programming. What did that leave? It was easy to eliminate some listings like those for lawyers, medical positions, and engineers. But she was still left with way too many pages and nothing that sounded promising or exciting.

Maybe Tiffany was searching in the wrong place.

Chris lived north of her in Dahlonega. What if she started her search in his area? Maybe she should find out how he felt about that.

She grabbed her cell phone and shot off a text. *I think I need more than a change in jobs.*

Chris replied immediately. *What does that mean? Are you dumping me?*

This wasn't a conversation for a text. She hit the call button.

Chris picked up on the first ring. "What's going on?"

"Of course I'm not dumping you."

"Then what are you talking about?" he asked.

"I'm thinking about moving."

"I can understand why you'd want to be closer to your aunt right now," Chris said.

"Not to South Carolina. Actually, I was thinking somewhere closer to home." Tiffany took a deep breath. "Like Dahlonega. That is, if you don't mind and if there are any jobs and apartments."

"Why would I mind?" Chris asked. "We could be together every day when I'm home. I miss you so much."

"Me too."

"I want to talk to you after this deployment."

"About what?" she asked, suddenly uneasy.

"My career," he said. "I'm wondering what you think I should do. If I should stay in the Army or get out."

"I thought you loved your job," Tiffany said, surprised.

"I do," Chris replied, "but I love you more."

"If I said I hate you going away, you'd get out?"

"Yes," he said without hesitation.

"I don't know if I could ask that of you," she admitted.

"You don't need to decide yet. Which is why I said I want to talk about it when I get back, but it wouldn't hurt for you to start thinking about it now." Chris laughed. "I was going to wait to bring it up when you got home from South Carolina, but you beat me to it."

"I've had a lot of time to think the past couple of days," Tiffany said. "I can't return to my old life. It's gone, and I can no longer pretend like nothing's changed. The idea of going home to the same apartment and the same job makes me want to cry."

"Then don't," he said. "I'm not sure what kinds of jobs are available here, but you can stay in my apartment while you check them out. You won't even have to worry about rent, because it's already paid for. That way you can take your time and find something you really want."

"I can't do that. I'm not going to take advantage of you."

"You're not. I offered," Chris reminded her. "Besides, if you stay here, then I'll know the place is being taken care of. It'll finally feel like a home to come back to."

Her head was swirling. There was so much to take in. Her mom gone. A new aunt. Searching for a new job, a new home, and now, maybe a new life with Chris. Not all of it was bad, but it was a lot to handle at once.

"Can I think about it and let you know?" Tiffany asked.

"I'd be worried if you answered right away. Take all the time you need. I miss you."

"I miss you too. I'll see you Saturday."

After Tiffany hung up, she hugged Winston. Despite the recent events, she couldn't stop grinning. She was anxious to share her conversation with Melinda and Laura. If only Melinda didn't have a headache and if only she were closer with Laura. Tiffany had traveled to South Carolina to meet her long-lost aunt, but it felt like she'd met two. She'd come to this inn an orphan, alone in the world, and now she was once again surrounded by friends and people who cared about her.

For now, she'd settle for her furry friend, which was fine as Winston was the best of company. "You know what?" she asked the dog. "I've never been so excited and scared in my life. Chris and I are both thinking of a future together. I just hope we make the right decision."

Winston lifted his head and licked her chin as if he understood, and Tiffany had no doubt the little dog actually did.

17

Melinda

Thursday morning, Melinda sat up straight in bed and smiled. "I've got it."

She jumped out of bed, threw open the French doors, and walked out onto the veranda to greet the day. After months of searching and applying for jobs and being rejected, she'd finally figured out a solution. But first, she had work to do.

She took a few deep breaths of the cool morning air and ran through a couple of yoga stretches, then marched back into her room and grabbed some clothes from the closet.

As soon as she was showered and dressed, she checked the hours for the local library. She still had time to eat one of Charlotte's mouthwatering breakfasts before heading into town.

"Good morning," Melinda called out to her hostesses when she entered the dining room. She picked up a plate from the sideboard and began to dish out scrambled eggs with ham, cheese, and chives. She filled the rest of the plate with bacon, a muffin, and fresh fruit.

"You seem much better this morning." Charlotte offered her a cup of coffee and a smile. "Did the tea help last night?"

"Yes, it did," Melinda said. "I slept great and woke up with all this energy. I feel like I could run into town."

"Well, the bicycle is available if you'd rather use it," Grace said.

Winston followed the three women out to the veranda and sat quietly next to Melinda's chair, gazing longingly into her eyes.

"Good morning to you, Winston." Melinda gestured at the other empty chairs. "Did I already miss Tiffany and Ryan?"

"I'm afraid so," Grace said. "Tiffany was up at the crack of dawn, went for a run, and left before seven. Ryan left right after that for a meeting with his client."

"Sounds like things are progressing well with her aunt and with Ryan's project," Melinda commented. "Is everyone staying until Saturday?"

"Yes, you're all booked until then," Grace replied.

"Maybe we could have some kind of farewell hospitality hour on Friday night," Melinda suggested. "A little something extra to celebrate a great week. I'd be happy to pay for the extra service, of course."

"That's a good idea, but there's no extra charge," Charlotte said. "I'll make a special dessert. As a matter of fact, it's the perfect excuse for me to test out a new recipe." She grinned. "If you don't mind being my test subject."

"I don't mind at all," Melinda said. "Everything you've made for us has been beyond delicious. Which reminds me, I'd love to take home one of your cookbooks. Could you add that one with the lovely cover of the inn to my bill, please?"

"Of course," Charlotte said. "I hope you'll enjoy it."

"What's on your agenda today?" Grace asked Melinda.

"I'm heading over to the library to do some research for an idea I had. If it pans out, I may have solved my job dilemma." Melinda lifted her coffee cup to her lips and smiled. It would be so nice to have a career again.

"That sounds exciting," Grace said. "And a little mysterious. Do we get any clues?"

Melinda laughed. "Not yet. But your aunt helped me figure it out."

"That doesn't surprise me at all," Charlotte said. "Winnie always knows what a person needs at just the right time."

Melinda finished the last of her breakfast and pushed away from the table. "I'll tell you more when I get back tonight. I want to make sure I have everything planned out before I spill the beans."

"Good luck," Grace said.

"I think I'll take you up on your offer to use the bike," Melinda said. "Since I'll be inside most of the day, it'll give me a chance to get some exercise."

"That's a great idea," Charlotte told her. "Let us know how it goes." She and her sister headed back inside with Winston on their heels.

Melinda grabbed her bag and walked outside to find the bicycle leaning against the tree in the front yard. She dropped her bag into the basket, jumped on the bike, and headed to town.

It was easy to find the Heritage Library, a two-story brick building with tall arched windows, marble steps, and a majestic entrance located a block over from Main Street. Melinda parked the bike and climbed the steps.

An older gray-haired woman with sharp blue eyes sat behind the circulation desk. She smiled at Melinda and introduced herself as Phyllis Gendel. "Please let me know if I can help you with anything."

Melinda approached the desk. "Actually I'm looking for some books on choosing a career and personality tests. Also, if you have any books on writing a business plan, those would be a big help."

"Are you asking for your son or daughter?" Phyllis asked. "If so, they really should check the books out themselves."

Melinda smiled, ready for that assumption. "No, the books are for me."

"Are you new to town? I don't believe I've seen you in here before." Phyllis got up from her desk and signaled for Melinda to follow.

"I'm a guest at the Magnolia Harbor Inn," Melinda answered. The next thing she knew, she was telling the librarian her whole story, which was odd. Before coming on this trip she'd never been much of a sharer.

Phyllis removed several books from the shelves and carried them to a table in the corner. "Let me know if you need anything else."

Melinda shook her head as she watched the woman hustle back to the front of the library. The poor thing. She hadn't asked for Melinda's life story. Staying at the inn had certainly made Melinda more talkative. But given what she was considering as a new career, maybe that was a good thing.

Over the next several hours, Melinda pored over one book after another. She took multiple personality tests and matched her results up with their ideal career choices. Apparently, accounting was perfect for her personality. She sighed. That was the last thing she wanted to hear.

Most jobs in the business, finance, and math sector were also well suited for her. More of life in an office. She'd also be a good fit for a career in the sciences and health care, except she got light-headed at the sight of serious injuries.

Many of the other jobs were in architecture, engineering, and computers, and they would require more schooling. Melinda would gladly leave that world to Tiffany.

Thankfully, her idea didn't land on the list of careers to avoid, which was probably more important. She felt a little more hopeful when she noticed a few jobs from the arts, design, and communications section were considered perfect matches for her.

Melinda was about to dive into the next book when her phone rang. She quickly answered to avoid interrupting the other library patrons.

"It's Ryan. Are you feeling better today?"

Now she wished she'd taken the time to check her caller ID, or better yet, silenced her phone when she entered the library. She wasn't sure she was ready to talk to him. "I am. Thank you for asking."

"That's good. I was worried when you didn't attend hospitality hour last night. If you're not busy, perhaps I can take you out to lunch."

Melinda glanced at the table with her notes and books scattered everywhere. If she left now, she'd lose her momentum. "I'm sorry, but I'm in the middle of a project. Maybe we can catch up later."

"Sure. Good luck with your project." Ryan disconnected.

Melinda's good mood deflated. She really liked Ryan and hated hurting his feelings. But she needed to get this work done before she headed home. Plus, she was doing him a favor whether he liked it or not, because spending time with someone who resembled his dead wife couldn't be healthy.

Another thought entered her mind. Ryan might have been upset because she hadn't shared what she'd been working on. She understood, but when she finished, she would explain everything. Hopefully she could share it with everyone this evening at hospitality hour.

Soon Melinda was back in the midst of books and plans. She lost track of time, not noticing people passing by or the sun dropping in the sky, until someone tapped her on the shoulder.

"The library is closing in ten minutes," Phyllis said. "I'm afraid since you're not a resident of Magnolia Harbor, I can't let you check out the books, but I can hold them for you, if you plan to return tomorrow."

Melinda glanced around, surprised at how fast the day had slipped by and how much work she still needed to do. "Actually, if I can make a few copies, I should be all set."

"Of course," Phyllis said. She helped Melinda gather the books, then made copies for her.

After Melinda thanked the librarian and left, she stopped at Cappy's pizza parlor and picked up a panini to go, knowing she wouldn't have time to go out for dinner. She was so close to finishing her business plan. If only she could get the numbers to balance.

As soon as she returned to the inn, she left a note on the reception desk for Grace and Charlotte, letting them know she wouldn't be attending hospitality hour, then went straight to her suite.

Melinda couldn't contain her excitement. At the small desk in the corner of her room, she spread out the sheet she'd been working on and booted up her laptop.

While she worked, she set the old mint tea tin next to her for inspiration and encouragement. Deep down, she knew that she was on the right track, but old habits were hard to break. Before she did something foolish, she needed to make sure the numbers backed up her ideas.

Once again, her phone rang. She checked the screen. It was Ryan.

"Hi," he said. "You don't have another headache, do you?"

"No, I'm fine. Just still working on this project, and I'm so close to finishing, I can taste it."

"Glad to hear it. Grace mentioned you had an idea for a new job."

"I do," Melinda answered. "As soon as I'm done, I promise I'll tell you all about it. I need to make sure it's going to work first."

"Can you take a break for dinner?" Ryan asked. "I saw a steak house a few towns over."

"That sounds good," she said, "but I already picked up something to eat."

"How about dessert?" he persisted.

Melinda scanned her notes. The budget for the first year was almost done, but she had only one day left in Magnolia Harbor, and she wanted to finish before she left. For her plan to work, she needed Tiffany on board, and she couldn't present a plan that was only partially complete. "Can we do lunch tomorrow instead? I'm so sorry. I really need to finish this tonight."

"Unfortunately, I'll be with my client all day," Ryan said, sounding disappointed. "Let's plan to meet up at hospitality hour tomorrow evening. Charlotte said we won't want to miss it."

After agreeing, Melinda disconnected the call and dived back into the numbers and the world she knew. If everything worked out with this new idea, she would be able to incorporate her accounting skills and her desire to work with people in a more flexible environment. It would be the best of both worlds. And if Tiffany was willing to join her, then she'd have a great business partner to boot.

The only thing that kept Melinda from being over the moon was knowing that things with Ryan wouldn't work out. She really liked him. She liked his sweet smile, quiet laugh, and easygoing manner. She liked the way she felt when she was with him—smart, interesting, funny, and captivating.

But now Melinda knew he wasn't seeing her but rather a ghost from his past.

And that was one thing she didn't know how to handle.

18

Tiffany

After a fitful night of sleep, Tiffany awoke feeling confident in her decision to relocate. She needed a fresh start, to be someplace where every park, store, restaurant, and person she passed didn't dredge up painful memories. Plus, being closer to Chris would allow them to spend more time together and see if they were ready to take their relationship to the next level.

After her talk with Winnie the other night, Tiffany also had a better understanding of her aunt's reluctance to discuss her mom. For now, she'd focus on stories that didn't involve her mom and dad, but eventually, if Laura was going to be a part of her life, she'd have to accept that her parents were very much a part of it too.

Tiffany walked out of her room to go to breakfast. She heard the door next to hers open and smiled when she saw Melinda. At last. She couldn't wait to share her phone conversation with her friend.

"I missed you last night," Tiffany said. "Are you all right?"

"I'm great," Melinda said, "but I want to talk to you for a minute."

If it wasn't for her friend's huge grin, Tiffany would have been concerned. Curious, she followed Melinda into her room.

Melinda paced back and forth, wringing her hands. "I've been waiting for you to get up for hours."

Tiffany knew Melinda had been spending a lot of time with Ryan lately, and her mind went straight for the obvious. "Don't tell me. Ryan has declared his undying love and asked you to marry him already." She held up her hands and laughed. "I knew you two were a perfect match the minute I saw you together."

Melinda stopped moving and stared at her. "What are you talking about? Of course he hasn't. I don't even know why you would say something like that."

"This doesn't have anything to do with you and Ryan?" Tiffany asked. She glanced around the room, trying to get a clue as to what was going on. There were papers all over the bed and desk, and clothes were strewn over the chairs. Whatever it was, Tiffany had learned that Melinda was a bit messy.

"No, this isn't about Ryan and me," Melinda said. "Actually, it's not going to work out between us, but that's another story."

"I'm so sorry," Tiffany said gently. She motioned to the papers and the open laptop and took another guess. "Did you find a clue to a secret treasure here in town?"

Melinda laughed. "This is even better."

"Okay, I give up," Tiffany said. "What are you talking about? What is all this mess about?"

"This is about me and you and work."

"I'm not following." Tiffany cleared a spot on the cluttered bed and sat down.

"Remember how we were talking the other day, and both of us said we weren't happy in our current professions?" Melinda asked.

Tiffany nodded. "You suggested I become a nanny."

"I've found a better option," Melinda said with a grin. She pointed to the laptop. "This is a business plan. I was up late writing it, making sure all the numbers added up and that it was feasible."

"What kind of business plan?" Tiffany felt Melinda's excitement, and she jumped off the bed and rushed over to the computer.

"Running our own event planning business."

Tiffany frowned. That was not the answer she'd expected. She was a software programmer. She didn't know the first thing about planning parties. But that wasn't really true. She'd been on the planning committee for her dorm in college. Most of it was common sense and having the right contacts. She had the first requirement.

"Tell me more." Tiffany sat down with the laptop and started reading.

Melinda outlined her plan. She went over start-up costs, expenses for the first year, and so on. She was definitely the numbers person.

"What do you think?" Melinda asked when she'd finished her pitch.

"I don't know," Tiffany said. "It's really different."

"Sure, it's out of our wheelhouse," Melinda said, "but that's what makes it so great. We both want something different. Plus, with our combined organizational skills, your computer skills, and my accounting skills and contacts, we'll have all the basics covered."

Tiffany had to admit that Melinda had a good point. The two of them brought a lot to the table. She scrolled down the business plan on the laptop. "I don't see anywhere in here that allows for office space."

"I thought we could run it out of my house for the first year," Melinda said. "It would help save on overhead until we're ready for a storefront. My house is big with plenty of space, and it's only about a thirty-minute drive from your place."

Tiffany flinched. In her shared excitement, she'd forgotten about her decision to move. "Actually, Chris and I had a conversation." She filled Melinda in on their call and her decision.

"I'm so happy for you," Melinda said. She opened a new tab on the computer and calculated the distance. "It's about an hour drive from Roswell to Dahlonega. That's not bad. We can do most of the work from our respective homes and commute only when we need to. Also, instead of focusing on the Atlanta market, we can focus farther north, where there's less competition."

"It sounds like you've thought of everything." Tiffany's resolve wavered. She did want something different, something flexible and fun. What was more fun than planning parties? But it might not be steady. Of course, she had savings, and when she sold her parents' place, that would add to her cushion. Maybe it was time to take a leap of faith. "You know what? I'm in."

"Really?" Melinda practically squealed. She gave Tiffany a big hug. "That's fantastic."

Tiffany laughed. "What's next?"

"We need to polish our business plan," Melinda said.

The two of them pushed the overstuffed chairs in front of the fireplace together and moved the bench from the foot of the bed to create a little table, then got to work.

Breakfast came and went, but neither of them cared. For the next several hours, they reread and refined their business plan. They shared ideas, they argued, and they laughed, but in the end, they finally agreed.

Around lunchtime, Tiffany had the feeling of being watched. She turned and gazed out the French doors. A small bird sat on the railing, chirping. She walked over to watch it. She had no idea why. As soon as she reached for the doorknob, the bird flew off to land on a branch of the big magnolia tree.

Tiffany spun around and grinned at Melinda. "I've got it!"

Melinda glanced up from her computer. "What?"

"Our company logo," Tiffany said, feeling a bit smug. "A magnolia tree."

"That's perfect," Melinda said. "A magnolia tree representing Magnolia Harbor where we met and this idea was born. Genius."

"Now we need a name," Tiffany said.

"How about M & T Event Management?" Melinda suggested.

"And I have an idea for company swag. We could give out tea tins with our logo on them. After all, that's how I came up with the name."

Tiffany blinked. "From a tea tin?"

"Yep." Melinda crossed the room to the desk, picked up an old mint tea tin, and handed it to Tiffany. "Winnie gave me this my first night here. I had no idea why, but clearly she knew it was exactly what I needed."

Tiffany ran her thumb across the lid. "You can see that it's a tin for mint tea. The only other letters you can easily read are *M* and *T*."

"Right. All I could think of when I saw it was Melinda and Tiffany, which made me think how easily we'd connected. I kept thinking how we were both searching for a new career, and then I began wondering if we should do something together. Event planning seemed like a good fit from our conversations and shopping trip. I know it sounds crazy, but I seriously think it'll work."

Tiffany laughed. "Agreed. Now, if I could find my mom's missing necklace, then I'd say this has been the perfect week."

After wrapping up a few more details and making plans for when they got home to set their new business in motion, the two parted, Melinda to get lunch and Tiffany to visit her aunt.

Despite the fact that her stomach rumbled in protest, Tiffany drove straight to Laura's house. She couldn't wait to share all her news with her aunt. If all of this had happened a year ago, Tiffany would have been on the phone with her mom. Since that wasn't possible, she talked with her on her drive, knowing that her mom was still watching out for her, just from a place much higher up.

As she pulled into Laura's driveway, her aunt was walking out the front door. Laura was dressed in dark pants, a button-down blouse, and a pair of ankle boots. Her long hair was swept into an intricate knot, and she wore makeup. It wasn't her normal outfit of worn jeans, a

T-shirt, and tennis shoes that Tiffany had grown accustomed to seeing.

Full of energy and excitement, Tiffany grabbed her purse and hopped out. They met at Laura's car.

"I didn't expect to see you today," Laura said. "I'm on my way out."

Tiffany stepped back, disappointed that she wouldn't be able to spend time with her aunt. "I'm sorry. I know we didn't make plans, but all this stuff has happened and I really wanted to talk to you about it." She smiled. "By the way, you look very nice."

"Thank you." Laura set her purse on the hood of the car and leaned back against it. "I've got a couple of minutes. Tell me what's got you all excited."

"I don't want to hold you up," Tiffany said.

"Nonsense. Spit it out."

Tiffany told her aunt about her call with Chris. While the new business venture was important, she really wanted Laura's take on her decision to move.

"Tell me one thing." Laura grasped the necklace hidden under her shirt. "When you and Chris are together, do you ever get tired of talking? Or do you feel like you could talk to him forever about anything and everything?"

Tiffany's mom had said something to her one time about finding the perfect match. She'd also mentioned never wanting the conversation to end, so Laura's question piqued her interest.

"I feel like even if we lived to be a hundred and ten, we'd still find something to talk about," Tiffany replied.

"Then it sounds like Chris is perfect for you."

"How do you know?"

"Your grandmother," Laura said. "That's how she knew your grandpa was the one. They could talk and talk and never grow bored of each other."

Tiffany didn't mention her mom or the fact that she'd said something similar years ago. "I hope I'm as lucky as Grandma." *And my mom.*

"It's a good goal." Laura checked her watch. "Was that all?"

"Well, there's this new business venture, but we can talk about that later." Tiffany started to walk away.

But her aunt stopped her. "I've got a few more minutes. Besides, I'm worried that if you don't tell me, you might burst."

Tiffany smiled and related to her aunt everything she and Melinda had discussed about their new business. When she finished, she asked, "What do you think? Am I crazy?"

"You might be." Laura smiled. "But only in the best kind of way. I think you're brave and smart, and now is the ideal time to break out and try something new. You're still young enough to find something else if this doesn't work out, but you're old enough to have a good head on your shoulders, so I think you should go for it."

"It's not too much all at once, is it?" Tiffany asked.

"You're asking someone who moved to another state without a plan or knowing a single person," Laura said. "Now, when are you supposed to go back to Georgia?"

A sudden feeling of loss came over Tiffany as she realized she had less than twenty-four hours left, and she wouldn't be able to spend them with the person she wanted to the most. "I check out of the inn tomorrow."

"Why don't you come over in the morning? We can talk one more time before you hit the road." Laura reached out and hugged her. "Congratulations."

Tiffany promised to be over bright and early the next day. Even though she was disappointed about losing a day with her aunt, she was also filled with hope. Laura had embraced her. They were making progress. Sure, they were taking baby steps, but babies started slow, and before long, no one could keep up with them.

Tiffany waved goodbye to her aunt, then gazed skyward and closed her eyes. "Thanks, Mom. Thank you for sending me on this mission."

19

Grace

After searching for days for the elusive key, Grace had finally given up on finding it and cut the locks off the shed. She couldn't wait any longer. They had to prepare for Helen's surprise party that was set for tomorrow night. Thankfully, nothing else had gone missing, and they hadn't noticed any strangers around the inn, so it was most likely a case of misplacing the items.

Grace stood on a tall ladder, hanging the freshly laundered curtains from the rafters in the barn. "Would you please hand me the last curtain?" she asked her aunt.

Winnie gave it to her, then held the ladder. "When is the florist due to arrive?"

"Tomorrow afternoon." Grace draped the curtain over the rafter. "With this warm streak we've been having, we were afraid the flowers would wilt if she came any sooner."

"Good thinking," Winnie said.

Grace climbed down the ladder, then admired her handiwork. By the time they were done decorating, the place would resemble an upscale restaurant instead of a barn.

"Are you sure Charlotte doesn't need my help with the food?" Winnie asked.

"I'm sure," Charlotte said as she walked inside.

Winston followed her. After greeting Grace and Winnie, the dog trotted around the barn, investigating all the new smells.

"You're always welcome to keep me company while I cook

tomorrow," Charlotte told Winnie. "Most of the prep work is already done, but it'll be a busy day and I'll have both ovens going."

"Isn't that a lot to take on by yourself?" Winnie asked. "Catering a whole party?"

"I'm only handling the finger foods," Charlotte said. "Angel is bringing the cake, and Edible Delights is sending someone to help with serving for the night. It's not a big party—only about thirty people."

"That's good to hear," Winnie said. "You girls are always so busy."

"We like it that way." Charlotte grinned. "Besides, what else would I do on a Saturday night? Dean's working."

"Did you have a chance to do the guest rooms?" Grace asked her sister.

Charlotte nodded. "I'm not sure what happened, but Melinda's room was a mess, which was surprising. When she first arrived, not a single thing was out of place, not even a wrinkle in the bed. Today it reminded me of my teenage bedroom."

"Really?" Grace asked. "I hope everything is okay. Melinda has seemed pretty stressed over not finding a job and making a career switch, which I understand all too well."

"You didn't stress over leaving the firm," Charlotte said.

"Oh yes she did." Winnie chuckled. "Your sister ate a lot of ice cream at that time."

Charlotte gaped at Grace. "How did I not know that?"

"Because I didn't want you to worry," Grace said.

"You did a good job of hiding it," Charlotte said. "I hope Melinda figures things out. Based on the papers, she might have."

"You didn't snoop, did you?" Grace asked, shocked that her sister would invade a guest's privacy.

"Of course not," Charlotte replied. "I was gathering up the papers and couldn't help but see some of what was written. Big, bold words like *business plan* in all capital letters sort of stand out."

Grace covered her face and took a breath. "I'm sorry. I don't know why I would even think that you'd do something like that. Please forgive me."

"It's fine," Charlotte assured her. "I know you're stressed. It's been a long week, and you've been worried about Tiffany's missing necklace and the lost key. Speaking of missing items, have you seen my little gold hoop earrings?"

"Not since you were wearing them a few days ago," Grace said.

"I thought I put them on my little entranceway table when I got home the other night," Charlotte said. "But when I looked last night, they weren't there. This morning, I hunted all over the cottage and couldn't find them."

"Did you check the kitchen?" Winnie asked.

"Yes, but they weren't there either," Charlotte said.

Grace pressed her fingertips to her forehead against the pressure building. What in the world was going on? How could so many miscellaneous things go missing? "This makes no sense."

Winston, sensing her distress, came over and put his paws on her knee.

Grace bent down to scratch his ears and ruffled his fur so her faithful friend would know she was all right.

"Perhaps you have a mischievous ghost," Winnie joked.

Charlotte laughed. "Well, if we do, I wish she'd return my earrings. Those were my favorites."

Grace dropped into one of the chairs and shook her head, frustrated and confused. Winston took that as an invitation and jumped into her lap. She snuggled him in her arms as she thought about the missing items. A key and a thimble were small random things she could have easily set down somewhere odd and forgotten about. However, she couldn't see a guest losing a sentimental necklace or Charlotte misplacing earrings she regularly wore.

"When Jake was little, he used to play jokes like this, but we haven't had any kids here lately," Charlotte remarked as she started moving tables around for the party.

After one last ear scratch, Grace set the dog down and got up to help. There was no point in losing valuable time stewing over something she couldn't figure out.

"I'm sure you'll find everything when you least expect it." Winnie covered the tables with fresh white tablecloths. "That's what happens to me."

"I hope you're right," Grace said.

"I was thinking that since everyone was checking out tomorrow, it would be a nice day for a family lunch," Winnie said.

"I can't," Charlotte said. "I've got to finish the prep for the party."

"Hear me out." Winnie smoothed one of the tablecloths. "You won't have to do anything."

Charlotte smiled. "I like this idea."

"Paisley and I will handle lunch," Winnie continued. "We'll cook and bring everything over here, so you won't have to take much time away from your kitchen. It's supposed to be gorgeous out, so I was thinking a picnic. It'll make for a quick cleanup. Dean can come because it's during the day. Surely he can take a short break and turn over the kitchen to one of his employees. And you'll invite Spencer too, Grace."

"That sounds lovely," Grace said. It had been a while since they'd had a real family get-together. It was a shame that Jake and the rest of the family lived so far away. She wished they could all join them.

"I'll call Dean as soon as we're done in here." Charlotte hugged Winnie. "Thank you for always being here for us."

"I'll second that," Grace said. She also gave her aunt a hug and then went back to work on setting up for the party. "I'm sure Spencer will be more than happy to come, especially if I tell him you're making potato salad."

"Of course I am," Winnie said. "What kind of picnic would it be without potato salad?"

"A very sad one," Charlotte said. "But thankfully, we don't have to worry about that."

"No, we don't," Grace said. "We only need to worry if anything else goes missing before everyone checks out tomorrow. Maybe we should keep the missing earrings quiet until then. We don't want to upset our guests."

"Ryan and Melinda haven't mentioned losing anything," Charlotte reminded her. "Besides, there's a good chance Tiffany lost her necklace before she even arrived. I wouldn't worry too much about it."

"But where are the key and my thimble?" Grace persisted. "And where are your earrings and measuring spoon? I'm afraid to keep searching and discover something else has disappeared."

"I'll come over this week and give each room a good, thorough cleaning." Winnie patted her arm. "Don't worry. We'll find everything. Probably right in front of our noses."

"Thanks," Grace said. "Maybe a new set of eyes is exactly what I need."

"Speaking of right in front of our noses, did Ryan say anything about Melinda last night?" Charlotte asked.

Grace raised her eyebrows. "What do you mean?"

"They seemed to be getting close, and then she suddenly closed herself off," Charlotte said as she set bud vases on each table.

"He didn't say anything to me," Winnie said.

"Me either," Grace said. "He talked about the project he landed and how we'd probably see him again soon, but he didn't say anything about Melinda. I didn't get the feeling that they got into a fight, but when Tiffany mentioned her name, he looked . . ."

"What?" Charlotte asked when she hesitated.

"Sad. Maybe a little disappointed." Grace shrugged. "I know she resembles Beth, but their personalities are very different. Maybe he was hoping they'd be more alike."

Even though Grace had been wary of Ryan and Melinda as a couple, it was a shame. When Grace had seen them at the festival, they'd seemed like such a good fit. They'd been happy and in sync with each other, like two halves finally come together. It had reminded her of how she felt when she was with Spencer.

"I think you just need to give them some time," Winnie said absently as she finished with the tables.

"You're not going to play matchmaker, are you?" Charlotte asked, crossing her arms over her chest. "Ryan has been through so much already."

"You know I never stick my nose where it doesn't belong," Winnie said, a twinkle in her eyes.

Charlotte shot Grace a knowing smile.

They both knew their aunt too well. If Winnie thought someone needed a nudge, she was always willing to provide it.

"I think we're set for now," Grace said, stepping back to regard the barn. "We've tested the lights, and everything works. At night it'll be like hundreds of stars overhead. Tomorrow the DJ will be here to set up and the florist will deliver the flowers. The wine is chilling. Spencer is picking up ice, and you've got the food covered."

"Why don't we go to the house and enjoy a light lunch before I start cooking again?" Charlotte asked.

Winston must have heard the word *lunch*, because he came running.

At the doorway, the women stopped to examine the barn one last time to make sure they hadn't missed anything.

As Grace turned back around, a bright glint of light blinded her. "What was that?"

"What?" Charlotte asked.

"Up there." Grace pointed at the magnolia tree. "Something shiny caught the sunlight. I'm going to go see what it is."

They trudged up the yard to the big tree, with Winston at their heels, and glanced up. The sun hit the mystery item again, but they couldn't make it out from where they stood. It was too high.

"Let me grab the ladder." Charlotte raced to the barn and returned with the ladder they'd been using to hang the curtains.

They leaned the ladder against the tree, and Grace climbed it. When she reached the right branch, she found a bird's nest and started laughing.

"Well, what is it?" Winnie asked.

"You're never going to believe this," Grace said.

A bird on a nearby branch squawked indignantly at her. Clearly, she was invading his or her space.

"You're killing me with the suspense," Charlotte said.

"Mystery solved." Grace held up a necklace that had been dangling on a small branch over the nest. "I'm pretty sure this is Tiffany's. Hang on a second." She pocketed the other items and climbed down before the bird got really territorial.

When Grace arrived safely on the ground, she removed the items from her pocket. "Here are your earrings, Charlotte. And our missing key." She'd also found a couple of tea candles, some change, her thimble, and a measuring spoon.

"How did they get up there?" Winnie asked.

Grace pointed to her feathered friend. "We have a thieving magpie."

All three laughed as they followed Winston to the inn.

"I know there was a tear in Tiffany's window screen, which explains how he got into her room, but how did he get the rest?" Winnie asked.

"It's been so nice this week, he probably snuck inside when we had the doors open," Grace said.

"I was airing out the cottage yesterday." Charlotte grinned and linked her arm through Grace's. "And here I thought all that time you spent reading Nancy Drew books was a waste."

"Reading is never a waste of time," Grace told her with a smile.

20

Melinda

Standing at the top of the stairs, Melinda took a deep breath and exhaled. Finally, she could breathe again. After months of struggling and feeling like she had been lost in a maze, she had finally found her way out and to the prize.

Earlier she'd taken a trip into town to grab a light snack at the Dragonfly Coffee Shop. Then she had called her parents and told them about her business idea and plan. They were thrilled. Her mom had a friend who needed help with a retirement party. Melinda hadn't even filed for her business license, and they already had a client lined up. It was a promising start.

She sailed down the stairs, feeling as light as air and grinning from ear to ear. As she stepped onto the back veranda, her breath caught. Charlotte and Grace had strung up fairy lights, and the tables were set with tablecloths and flowers. Upbeat music played in the background, and the scent of bacon wafted through the air.

Initially, Melinda had thought that tonight would be a little farewell party for her and Ryan and Tiffany. After all, they had hit it off right away, and it seemed fitting to end the week with a bang of sorts. But now, they had so many things to celebrate, including Melinda and Tiffany's new business venture, the friendship the three of them had formed, Ryan's work contract, and Tiffany's developing relationship with her aunt.

It was amazing what a week could accomplish. Melinda had a plan for a new career, a purpose in life, and new friends. She felt like a million bucks.

She couldn't wait to share the news with her hostesses and Ryan, but no one else was on the veranda. "I wonder where everyone is," she mused aloud.

Charlotte appeared with a tray of chocolate cupcakes, along with a plate of cheese and crackers. "Tiffany just got back. She said she'll be down in a few minutes." After setting the food on the buffet table, she turned to Melinda. "I think Ryan is taking a walk."

"Everything looks amazing."

"Thank you," Charlotte said.

"Will Grace be joining us tonight too?" Melinda wanted everyone to hear her big announcement. Grace had been so kind to Melinda, and she couldn't imagine having the party without her.

"She will," Charlotte said. "She and Winnie are in the kitchen finishing up a few things. Both should be out soon."

"Great." Melinda glanced toward the lake. "If you don't mind, I'm going to take a couple of wineglasses and go look for Ryan. We haven't had much time to talk recently."

"Not at all. If you want to lure him to the party, tell him I made bacon-wrapped shrimp." Charlotte winked and went back inside.

Melinda filled two glasses, then descended the steps and crossed the lawn. The sun was sinking into the western sky, leaving slashes of dusky pink, smoky purple, dark orange, and a hint of yellow. It was the kind of evening to sit with someone special and simply appreciate all that life had to offer. Her mind immediately went to Ryan, and she hated the idea that this would be their last sunset together.

She had hoped . . . Well, it didn't matter now.

Melinda spotted Ryan by the dock, skipping stones. For a moment, she stood and watched. He tossed one stone after another. Some skipped a few times before sinking, and others made a big splash before disappearing beneath the lake's dark surface. Then his shoulders slumped, and he stuck his hands into his pockets. Ryan reminded her of how she'd felt when she'd arrived in Magnolia Harbor—lost, alone, and in need of a friend.

Melinda approached him. "I brought you something, but if I'm interrupting your quiet time, I can leave." She held out a wineglass, hoping he'd accept.

"Thanks," Ryan said as he took the glass. "I was thinking about getting a drink."

"Great minds think alike," she said. "Bad day?"

"Long day," he said. "How about you? Did you finish what you were working on? No more headaches?"

"The headaches are all gone." Melinda walked over to a bench and took a seat. "I'm done with my project. Or rather, I'm beginning it."

"That sounds intriguing." Ryan sat next to her, but he kept some space between them.

"I was going to wait for everyone to join us on the veranda, but I have to tell you." She launched into the story of how she came up with her business idea and that she and Tiffany would be partners. When she finished, she thought Ryan would be thrilled for her.

"That's great," he said, but his tone didn't support the sentiment.

"Thanks, but you don't sound very convincing." Melinda laughed lightly and nudged his arm with hers. "Is everything going okay with your new contract?"

"Work is fine. Well, we're butting heads a little, but that's to be expected." Ryan leaned forward, resting his forearms on his legs, and gazed at the lake. "I have a confession."

"Does it require the services of a priest?" Melinda joked.

"Not that kind of confession," Ryan said with a laugh. Then he turned serious. "I like you a lot."

"Ditto. I mean, I like you, not I like me, although I do like me too." She cringed. "I'm sorry. Sometimes I ramble when I get nervous."

"Why are you nervous?" Ryan asked, searching her face.

"Because I'm afraid of what you're going to say next." Melinda took his hand. "But I want to hear it."

"I think I'm falling for you," he said. "You're funny, smart, interesting, independent, adventurous, and you make me want to live my life again. But—"

"Why is there always a 'but'?" she interrupted.

"I don't know. To keep us on our toes, I suppose."

"Sometimes it isn't so bad to have your feet on the ground."

"No, it's not." Ryan squeezed her hand, then released it. "What I'm trying to say is that I feel like it's a one-way street. You see me as a friend, but what I'm hoping for could be so much more."

Melinda was stunned. She knew they had developed a special friendship, but she hadn't thought it would really go anywhere. Especially not after seeing the picture of his late wife.

Could Melinda have been wrong?

There was only one way to find out. Melinda plunged ahead. "I think we're standing on the same street, just opposite sides. I haven't met anyone in a long time who makes me as happy as you do."

"If we're on the same street, then why do I feel so alone?" Ryan asked. "You've been avoiding me and refusing my offers, like you learned some horrible secret about me."

Melinda bit the inside of her cheek and then blurted out the truth. "It was the picture of Beth."

"What about it?" he asked. "You knew I was widowed."

"I did, but I didn't know that I could be her understudy."

"What do you mean?"

"I like you very much," Melinda said, trying again. "But I've been worried that the only reason you're interested in me is because I resemble the woman you loved and lost. I can't be a substitute for her."

She blew out a breath. It felt good to be honest with Ryan and share her fears with him. She hadn't realized how much they had weighed her down.

If they had any hope of seeing if their friendship could develop into something more, they needed to talk about doubts and things that upset them. She knew that relationships could only survive if there was plenty of trust, honesty, and faith. Without them, love never stood a chance.

"To be honest, that was what originally caught my eye when I first saw you," Ryan admitted.

Even though Melinda suspected it, she couldn't deny how disappointed she was. Her celebratory mood vanished into thin air, leaving her with a feeling reminiscent of being punched in the gut.

"But within five minutes of talking to you, I no longer saw Beth when I looked at you," he continued. "I saw Melinda Rainey, one of the most captivating women I'd ever met. While you two have some physical similarities, you're very different people."

Relief washed over Melinda, but she was still torn. "I'm glad to hear that, but I'm also not sure I'm ready to start a relationship right now, what with this new business and all. Plus, we don't even live near each other."

"I'd drive across the country if I had to," Ryan said. "Thankfully, Athens is only about an hour and a half from Roswell."

"You make it sound so simple."

"It is, and if you took that bookkeeping position with me, we'd have even more time together. I want to be an open book. No secrets. No more doubts."

"Here's the deal," Melinda said, deciding to take a chance. "I'll work for you until my business takes off. That will give us time to get to know each other better. But from here on out, no holding things in, no suppressing our emotions—good or bad." She held out her hand. "Deal?"

"Deal," Ryan said as he shook it. Then he wrapped her in a tight hug and held her for a moment. "If you're free, I'd like to come to Roswell next weekend and spend the day with you."

"Or I could drive to Athens," Melinda offered.

"We'll talk about it this week," he said. "Tonight let me take you out to dinner to celebrate your new career, because I don't want to wait a week for our next date."

"That sounds great, but I have a little surprise for you and Tiffany," Melinda said. "Come on."

When they arrived at the veranda, Winston bounded over to greet them. Grace, Charlotte, and Winnie were huddled around one of the tables with Tiffany.

"Looks like the gang is all here now," Melinda said. "What's going on?"

"Grace found my necklace." Tiffany held up a long chain, tears glimmering in her eyes. "Now I can complete my mom's final wish."

"Oh, that's wonderful news." Melinda hurried over and gave her new friend and business partner a hug. She knew how much it meant to Tiffany to be able to carry out her mother's dying request. "Where was it?"

"You're not going to believe this." Grace chuckled. "We had a thieving magpie. He also snatched my key to the shed."

"And my earrings," Charlotte added. "Along with several other things."

While Grace filled Melinda and Ryan in on how they'd discovered their feathered foe and rescued the stolen items, Winnie refreshed everyone's wine.

"It's a good thing we planned a party." Melinda raised her glass. "I'd like to make a toast to new friends—including you, Winston—creating new bonds, and embarking on new adventures."

"Cheers!" the others cried, clinking their glasses.

Not to be left out, Winston yipped, then danced in a circle.

"New adventures?" Grace asked, lifting one brow. "That sounds intriguing."

"It's simply fabulous," Tiffany said, then turned to Melinda. "Tell them about our business venture."

Melinda filled the rest of the group in on the news, then removed the old mint tea tin out of her pocket. She explained the role it had played, including their new business name and logo design.

Everyone agreed it was a great name and idea.

"I especially owe you a huge thank-you," Melinda said to Winnie. "Your gift was quite the muse."

"I'm so glad to hear it came in handy." Winnie smiled and sipped her wine, a knowing sparkle in her eyes.

21

Tiffany

Saturday morning, Tiffany checked out of the Magnolia Harbor Inn. She thanked Grace and Charlotte and spent some time cuddling with Winston. She was going to miss all three of them, and she hoped it wouldn't be the last time she saw them.

Tiffany was excited when she drove to her aunt's house. After pulling into the driveway, she sat in her car for a few minutes. A sense of déjà vu came over her. Had it been only five days since she'd first sat here and stared at the house before her? It had definitely been an interesting trip. When Tiffany had set out to grant her mother's request, she hadn't expected to return home with a new family member, new friends, and a new career.

For the first time in months, she was actually looking forward to getting on with her life. Tiffany would always miss her mother. She'd miss their talks, her hugs, and her advice. She'd miss her smile and voice and unconditional support, especially when she needed it the most. But her life had to go on. Otherwise, she would truly let her mother down.

Donna Devereux Jackson had never given up on life, not even at the end, and she wouldn't want her daughter to give up either.

So starting today, Tiffany vowed she would live the best life she could. She'd fill it with purpose, laughter, and love, and she'd share it all with friends and family. Her mom would always be a part of her, forever etched in her heart.

Finally, Tiffany gathered up her purse, double-checked that she had the necklace, and got out of the car.

"It's about time," Laura said from her chair on the porch. "I thought you might be planning to sit in your car all day."

Tiffany smiled and took the chair opposite her.

Laura poured her a cup of hot tea.

They sat in silence for a few minutes, simply enjoying the cool morning air scented with the last of the season's flowers from her aunt's yard. There was something special about Saturday mornings when there was no need to rush. Except today Tiffany got the feeling they were both trying to extend their time together for as long as they could.

Tiffany took the necklace out of her purse and set it on the table between them. "I didn't lose it after all. Just lent it to a magpie for a little while."

"Someday I'll ask you to explain but not right now," Laura said. As she picked up the necklace, tears ran down her cheeks. Slowly, with her other hand, she drew out the necklace that was hidden beneath her shirt and showed it to Tiffany.

This was the first time Tiffany had seen her aunt's necklace. It matched the one her mother had. It was a gold arrow with an amethyst.

"Your mom and I got these from our parents on our sixteenth birthday," Laura said between her sniffles. "It's our birthstone."

"All this time, I never realized it was Mom's birthstone," Tiffany said, surprised.

"Did you see the initials?" Laura asked.

Tiffany peered closer and saw the initials *DMD*. Donna Marie Devereux. She couldn't believe that she'd never noticed them before. Then again, her mother had never taken off the necklace or allowed Tiffany to examine it. "Those are my mom's initials."

Laura nodded, then held up Tiffany's mother's necklace. "And these are mine."

"LAD," Tiffany said.

"Laura Ann Devereux."

"That's amazing," Tiffany said.

"That night on our birthday, we exchanged necklaces and promised we'd wear them always," Laura continued. "So no matter where the other was, we were always together. I've never taken it off since."

Tiffany couldn't stop the tears from falling. "Mom never did either."

It finally made sense why her mother had never taken off the necklace and why it had been so important for Tiffany to give it to Laura. Her mother had chosen to live her life with the man she loved, but she'd never stopped loving her sister.

Tiffany had reunited the sisters at last.

"I assumed your mom would have gotten rid of the necklace a long time ago," Laura said as she rubbed her thumb back and forth over the initials. "I'm glad I was wrong."

"Mom never mentioned having a sister, so finding out about you was a shock to say the least," Tiffany said. "I think it hurt her too much to talk about you, but I know she loved you."

"How can you be sure if she never even talked about me?" Laura asked.

"You were the last person she thought about before she passed away. Not my dad. Not me. It was you."

They sat in silence for a few minutes, Tiffany's words hanging in the air between them.

"Can you do me a favor?" Laura asked at length.

Tiffany nodded, ready for whatever new quest was given to her.

"Would you keep this necklace and wear it?"

"I can't do that," Tiffany said. "It's yours. My mom wanted you to have it."

"Please take it." Laura pressed the necklace into Tiffany's hand. "I need you to remember that wherever you go, not only is your mother with you, but so am I."

Tiffany slipped the necklace over her head, then grabbed a napkin to dry her eyes. If she stayed any longer, she'd be too much of an emotional wreck to drive, so she stood. "I should get going."

Laura gazed at the necklace Tiffany now wore. "I wish you'd stay a little longer. Let us talk and really get to know each other." She smiled. "I could tell you some good stories about your mother before she was a wife and a mom."

Tiffany latched on to that smile. One she'd missed so dearly. "I've got some time."

Laura rose. "Let's go inside while I make us some fresh tea."

Tiffany followed her aunt into the kitchen. This time, she didn't bother to ask to help. Instead, she sat down at the old worn table.

"I owe you an apology," Laura said as she filled the teakettle and put it on the stove. "I know you've been trying to get to know me, to connect with a person who should love you unconditionally, and I've been standoffish."

"It's okay. I'm sure I was a surprise to you."

Laura leaned against the counter. "It's true you were a shock, but I was so filled with grief that I couldn't let any other emotions in."

Tiffany didn't know what to say. Been there, done that? No, it was better to be quiet for once and let Laura talk. Besides, Tiffany had already said everything she needed to say. Now it was her aunt's turn.

"A person always thinks they have plenty of time," Laura said. "Time to right the wrongs and make up with loved ones. I always believed that's what would happen with your mom. I was sure that someday one of us would find the other, and we'd mend this silly rift."

The teakettle whistled, and Laura poured fresh tea into their mugs, then sat down at the table across from Tiffany. Neither one of them touched their tea.

"When you showed up, it made me realize time had run out," Laura continued. "I was mad at myself, mad at your mother. How could she leave me here? We came into this world together. We should be leaving it together, and I've got no plans to do that for another forty or more years."

Tiffany laughed. She could see that her aunt didn't know how to quit any more than she or her mom did.

"I was also mad at your father," Laura admitted. "I've been mad at him for thirty years, so that was nothing new. But I was mad at you too, because if you hadn't shown up, I could have gone along pretending I didn't care that I'd lost my sister all those years ago."

"I'm so sorry." What else could Tiffany say? That she'd rather pretend she hadn't lost her mother too? She was pretty sure Laura knew that already. That she hadn't meant to upset Laura's carefully constructed life? But she couldn't regret that she had done so, because now she wasn't alone. They had each other.

The two talked, hugged, and cried. Laura broke out a coffee cake she'd made for them, and they dug in as Laura told her stories about her mom as a child and a teen. Contrary to what her mother had told her, she hadn't been an angel. Tiffany laughed over the twins' antics in school, switching places and pretending to be each other.

Tiffany cherished every moment with her aunt. She enjoyed every tale, every memory. She'd lost track of how many times one or the other broke down crying, sharing their grief and love for the woman who had brought them together.

As morning made way for afternoon, Tiffany knew her time was coming to a close. She'd promised Chris she'd be home tonight, and he had only a short time left before he deployed. It was just as important for them to have that time together as it was for her to have this time with her aunt to truly bond.

Tiffany stood and stretched before carrying the empty cake plates to the sink.

Laura joined her and pulled her in for a fierce hug.

"Thank you for today," Tiffany said. "Thanks for telling me everything you were going through. I understand the anger. Maybe too well. I might not be able to imagine being in either of your shoes all those years ago or understand it, but I'm glad I have you now."

"I wish you could stay here with me so we could have more quality time together," Laura said. "But I understand that you need to get home. See your boyfriend and get to work on your new business." She smiled. "You're always welcome here. I want you to consider this your second home."

"I will," Tiffany said. "Maybe you can visit me in Atlanta or Dahlonega or wherever it is I land. You can meet Chris. We could spend the holidays together."

Laura gave her another hug. "I can't think of anywhere else I'd rather spend them."

22

Grace

It was only nine thirty on Saturday morning, and Grace was ready for a nap. She'd been up since five, and she'd helped Charlotte with breakfast, checked out two guests, and cleaned their rooms so they were ready for the next guests to check in. Thankfully, no one was scheduled to arrive until after four, during which time she had a florist to oversee as well as the DJ. She still had one room left to clean, but Melinda didn't appear ready to check out, and Grace had no wish to hurry her along.

She popped into the kitchen, where Charlotte was surrounded by pots, pans, and bowls as she prepared for tonight's party. "Do you need a hand?"

"Not in here," Charlotte answered. "You can see if Melinda would like any more coffee or muffins. She's out on the back veranda."

"No problem." Grace grabbed the coffeepot and a basket of fresh apple-pear cinnamon muffins and headed outside, where she found Melinda lost in thought. "Can I get you a refill?"

Melinda peered into her cup. "Just half a cup. Otherwise, I might not sleep until next week. It'll be my fourth cup today."

Grace set the muffins on the table and took the chair next to her so they both could gaze at the lake that was as pretty as smoked glass. "It's a perfect spot to sit, relax, and think."

"It is." Melinda sighed. "I should get out of your hair and head home. I'm sure you've got a ton of guests to get ready for, and you have that party tonight."

"There's no rush," Grace assured her. "Checkout isn't officially for a while, and there's no sense cutting your vacation short." She studied her guest. "You seem a little melancholy this morning. Is everything okay?"

"It is." Melinda toyed with the coffee cup, a slow, shy grin forming. "It's been such a wonderful trip. When I arrived, I had no idea that I'd go home with an answer to my problem in addition to some wonderful new friends."

"You do seem more relaxed," Grace observed.

"I feel it too, which is weird. I should be stressed about the new business with Tiffany, but I'm so confident in our skills and drive that I'm simply excited."

"That's a great sign," Grace said. "It sounds like you're on the right track."

"I have you to thank for a lot of my current mood," Melinda continued. "You were so kind with your time and advice and your friendship. Creating that spreadsheet for you and Charlotte is what got the ball rolling."

News like this filled Grace with satisfaction and pride. Running the inn gave her a chance to fulfill a greater purpose by helping others—something that had been sorely lacking at the marketing firm. "I'm glad I was able to help."

"It's been a life-changing trip," Melinda said. "I've got a new career, a new hobby—Winnie introduced me to embroidery—and then there's Ryan."

"I'm thrilled to see that you two hit it off so well and that you're going to see each other again," Grace said. "Ryan's a wonderful man, and he deserves to be with someone equally wonderful, like you." She smiled. "I hope we'll see both of you the same time next year on his annual trip."

Grace kept to herself that she'd had doubts at the beginning—no one needed to hear that kind of talk when they were starting out in a relationship. Plus, after seeing the two together last evening at hospitality hour, she'd realized she'd been wrong in her initial thoughts.

"We'll have to see how we progress," Melinda said. "Either way, I'll be making my way back here. When will depend on a lot of things, like the new business."

"Of course, and if you ever need to talk, I'm here for you," Grace said. "I have a feeling you and Tiffany are going to be very busy and successful."

Melinda stood. "I can't thank you enough for the wonderful time, all your encouragement, and mostly for your friendship."

Grace caught a slight hesitation in Melinda's voice. She understood that starting over could be exhilarating as well as scary. She'd been there, had gone through all those emotions, and she could relate all too well.

"When you have multiple clients demanding your attention at the same time, deadlines looming, and suppliers running late or canceling, remember to breathe," Grace advised. "Take each day as it comes, whether you're focusing on your relationship with Ryan or your business. Tomorrow is always a fresh start. If you ever need a place to escape or recharge, you know the way to Magnolia Harbor."

Melinda laughed and hugged her before heading to her room to pack. She promised she'd stop by the kitchen to say goodbye to Charlotte and Winston.

After her guest and new friend left, Grace reflected on her life as she carried the remaining breakfast dishes to the kitchen. It seemed like only yesterday when Grace had been in Melinda's shoes. Changing careers and opening the inn with Charlotte had been a challenge, but it was also one of the best decisions she'd ever made. Grace loved what she did, so it no longer felt like work, a daily chore to handle, but rather a labor of love.

Grace stopped at the reception desk to check for messages. She heard a car pull into the driveway and peeked out the window. Winnie exited the car and carried two bags up the walk.

Grace opened the door for her aunt and took one of the bags out of her hands. "What's all this?"

"The first wave of food for the family picnic. That's my potato salad." Winnie raised the other bag. "And this is chocolate cherry cake with frosting. I've got more in the car too. Paisley and her family will be here at twelve thirty, but I wanted to come early to see if Charlotte needed my help."

"You know she'll refuse."

"I also know I can ignore her when she does," Winnie replied brightly.

Together they unloaded Winnie's car, then stored the perishables in the refrigerator.

Grace was putting the finishing touches—mint leaves and lemon—on a fresh pitcher of sweet tea when Winston scurried into the kitchen, whining.

"What's up, Winston?" Winnie asked.

"It sounds like Melinda is ready to check out," Charlotte said.

The three walked out to the foyer to find their last guest descending the stairs.

"I'm glad you're all here." Melinda set her suitcase down and picked up Winston. "I'm going to miss you and your morning snuggles, my little friend. You'll be happy to know you've inspired me to adopt a furry companion or two of my own."

Winston licked her chin.

After setting Winston down, Melinda hugged Grace and Charlotte, then took hold of Winnie's hands. "You're all so wonderful. I feel like I'm saying goodbye to old friends, not people I just met. This place is so much more than simply an inn, and you've made us feel like more than guests. You welcomed us into your home, and you're forever in my heart. Please know that if any of you make your way to Roswell, my door is always open."

By the time Melinda left, Grace wasn't the only one with tears in her eyes. Melinda's words had reached deep down into Grace's heart and soul. She had thanked Grace for her encouragement, but what Melinda didn't realize was that it was guests like her, Ryan, and Tiffany who not only encouraged Grace to keep her doors open but reaffirmed her choice.

Charlotte wiped the tears from her eyes and smiled at Grace. "Allergies," she claimed.

"Some people who pass through these doors are definitely hard to say goodbye to." Grace closed the door.

They headed to the kitchen, the heart of the home.

"Melinda was right," Winnie commented. "You two provide your guests with more than a place to lay their heads. You offer them a home away from home and your friendship—the most precious of all gifts. I'm so proud of you both."

"I believe she was talking about you too," Charlotte said as she slid a plate of fudge brownies onto the island in front of them.

"Those look so good," Winnie said. "But it's only ten in the morning, and I'm sure they'll send my blood sugar racing toward the sky."

Charlotte grinned. "First of all, it's snack time somewhere, and second, I made them with you in mind."

"In that case, I'm getting the whipped cream for mine," Grace announced. "We'll call it a mini-celebration for a job well done this week."

"Speaking of weeks," Winnie said, setting her brownie on a plate. "What's next?"

And with that, the three of them fell into their easy rhythm. Charlotte topped their brownies with whipped cream and filled their coffee mugs with fresh brew, Grace reminded them of who was checking in and when over the next week. Winnie noted the schedule and promised to be on hand to help. Winston went to bed, probably to nap and prepare for new guests to greet.

In other words, everything was perfect at the Magnolia Harbor Inn.